For a Girl
in a Star

For a Girl in a Star

Ratna Chandu

Srishti
PUBLISHERS & DISTRIBUTORS

SRISHTI PUBLISHERS & DISTRIBUTORS
Registered Office: N-16, C.R. Park
New Delhi – 110 019
Corporate Office: 212A, Peacock Lane
Shahpur Jat, New Delhi – 110 049
editorial@srishtipublishers.com

First published by
Srishti Publishers & Distributors in 2018

10 9 8 7 6 5 4 3 2 1

Dedicated to my Dad – a person with unflinching loyalty, who lived all his life without fanfare, taking care of my bed-ridden mother, and dreamed secretly about his daughter to reach the pinnacle of success, though he never breathed a single word. I hope you'd be proud now.

To my gleeful mother, who loves me, no matter what I do.

And last, but not the least, my husband, without whom the words would have died on the very first page.

Acknowledgements

Unlike the long list of acknowledgements, I'd like to offer my devout thanks to the significant person behind this book, my husband Chandu. He has always been the backbone and the lynchpin for every word that went into this book. What could I say about his unfathomable faith in me and drive! He's been lending his hand in every up and down, with an uncompromising stance to see this on a book shelf, all through. So, thank you my dear for having helped me recognize my hidden potential.

A special thanks to team Srishti Publishers and Arup Bose for giving me this opportunity.

It was probably one of the darkest nights. The power in the entire north lane had been out for the last couple of hours. The streets witnessed a deadly silence like never before. The moon hid behind thick clouds, intensifying the eeriness, and the lane looked haunted.

A small house sat at the corner of the wickedly dark lane. Inside, a tall man stood in front of the table lit by a single candle. He clamped his hands over his chest, his eyes glued on a drawing, admiring its flawless lines, which could be seen below the object on top of it.

The guy bent a little forward to get a perfect view.

It was a drawing of two boys, probably in their teens, who sat on a low cliff facing a waterfall. The foaming waters were streaming down the huge mountain. Though the boys' faces couldn't be seen, one could easily feel the laughter on their faces, their chins raised up in a warm chuckle. The drawing looked like a full moon. It was so vivid and real that it felt as if a long-lost moment had passed right in front your eyes. But a full moon had a dark side too, which only a few can see.

Suddenly, the guy was struck by strange nostalgia. In fact, whenever he saw any drawing, a similar emotion crawled in. "Isn't drawing in his blood? He can depict any beauty and experience on a piece of paper. But this specific drawing can be drawn at any time just from memory. He himself does not know how many times he has drawn this," the guy thought, his chest filled with immense pride and appreciation.

Outside, the deadly silence was interrupted by howling winds all of a sudden. They blew harder and harder, signalling the approach of a monstrous storm, and the arrival of something terrible. As expected, huge raindrops began to fall, turning the roads into rivers of mud, which had been parched dry minutes before, just the way fate changed in the flick of a moment.

Just then, a fast-moving dilapidated van came to a screeching halt, squirting a stream of dirty water on both sides. It stopped right outside the small house. The door slid open. A bunch of men stepped out hurriedly, their faces covered with bandannas. They made their way straight to the house and marched in through the open door. There was no one around to see the horror of what one man was carrying in his hands. It was a butcher's knife.

Inside the house, the guy could clearly hear the sound of footwear against the floor. But neither did he turn around to look, nor did he move an inch. Instead, he stood rooted in his place. Strangely, his eyes bore no sign of panic or fright, though a tear rolled down his cheek and fell on the drawing. The goons advanced closer to him. An average human being would jump to defend himself, but the guy stood there until it was too late, like he was anticipating their arrival.

Sooner, one of the goons approached him and gave a quick stab in his ribs. The razor-sharp knife smoothly sliced through his body, crushing thousands of nerve fibers. The other men stood back, all set to attack in case he made a counterattack.

But no! There was no retaliation from the guy yet.

He stood as if he had not taken a jab. But the pain was unbearable, making it impossible for him to breathe. Beads of blood sputtered down to the floor. And yet, he stood tall like an unflinching warrior, until another stab pierced his ribs. It was more forceful and intense than the previous one. Now, the guy's body shook like the fluttering candlelight that sat on the table, one of his hands clamped over the bleeding ribs. His legs nearly buckled, trembling. When he couldn't stand anymore, he collapsed on the floor with a heavy thud, his face down. Soon, he felt his breath leave him slowly.

One of them came forward and recklessly pushed his foot at the lifeless body and snapped his head around and nodded at other men, signalling it was to time to leave. Soon they all left the house in rush before someone caught them.

The guy lay on the floor in the pool of his own blood, his limbs strewn across in an impossible manner, motionless, for a very long time. His body shook with a coughing pit and he knew he wasn't going to make it. But strangely, his lips were curved in a quirky, mysterious smile. Could someone really smile at their own death, even if they had anticipated it? If so, how on earth could one anticipate their own death?

Soon, the fluttering candle went off. The rain outside came to a halt and it was dark again like before. The guy's eyelids began to droop until they stopped dead.

A few months back

It was a chilly morning in Bangalore. The temperatures had dropped drastically. Those were the days before the 1990s when only a few houses had fans. The cool air made the city feel as if it was air-conditioned under the open sky. The roads were empty. People were probably snuggling under thick blankets, snoring. The alarm rang in a cozy, small room for the second time. Avinash, who had lazily buried his head under a pile of two pillows, extended his hand to hit the snooze button and went back to sleeping. Grabbing those extra minutes of tempting sleep on dark mornings couldn't be replaced with any nectar. Damn! The entire city was doing that, he thought. Besides, he was never an early riser.

The alarm sang for the third time singing, "It's 5.00 a.m. Please wake up!" Avinash suddenly woke up, alerted, his hair tousled. He sat on his knees taking a moment before he jumped out of bed quickly.

And then, the rollercoaster ride started!

He quickly freshened up and raked a comb through his hair hastily, unlike Sundays when he spent ample amount of time carefully grooming it. Before leaving, he darted across the entire room like a manic, searching for something.

The floor was filled with a variety of objects, especially pencils – all types of HB's and H's, graphite sticks. Lying between them were large sheets of paper, some rolled and some spread out with drawings on them. There was a heap of wrinkled clothes, probably left unfolded for months, right in the middle of the room. At the corner was a small bookshelf where books had been literally dumped. The room looked like a little garbage dump. It was so messy that even a muddy pig would refuse to step in, saying that it would be an insult to live here.

Besides, what was he looking for? A helmet!

Yes, it was damn cold out there and he didn't want to freeze like a statue. But he couldn't find a helmet in the two-hundred-sq-ft room in which he had been living for years. Now he had to walk out without it since he couldn't afford to be late. The train would arrive at 5.30 at the station and his friend was new to the city.

Without a helmet, Avinash started his bike and sped down the dark street. As expected, the cold wind slapped against his face as if pieces of ice had been thrown at him. Within minutes, his hands and face turned numb. The biting cold was worse than he had expected and there were no people around. Amidst all this, his thoughts suddenly swung back to how he had ended up in Bangalore. Avinash was born and brought up in Agumbe, a small village located a few kilometres away from Bangalore. It was a tiny village, known for its plunging waterfalls and spectacular sunsets. Houses nestled under the thick branches of trees, looking as if they had emerged from them. The popular TV serial *Malgudi Days* had been picturized around there. Tourists thronged the town to trek and photograph its scenic beauty all the time.

Both Avinash's parents were farmers from the same village who cultivated crops of areca nut for a Brahmin landlord. Being poor Dalits, they couldn't afford to give their son a decent education, and so he was sent to a small school run by the village panchayat. Besides, Avinash was never a smart student, but was smart enough to bunk the school by making stupid excuses so that he could roam around the village. Despite his mischief, there was something about him that attracted everyone's attention. He was an artist. His love for drawing mesmerized people. He could recreate anything he saw, from creepy crawlies and the narrow waters jumping down the lush green hills, to the beautiful village girls. He could spend hours sitting on a tiny rock, with his hands making delicate strokes on a piece of paper. Everyone loved his drawings. After his schooling, his parents found it difficult to gather the money to educate him further. Moreover, he showed no interest in studying further. So they forced him to join them in the fields, hoping that their financial burdens would be lessened. But showing no interest in studies didn't mean that Avinash wanted to spend the rest of his life under the scorching sun and pelting rains in the fields. Although he had no clear picture of what he wanted to do in life, his heart always leaned towards the arts. So he decided to refine his god-gifted talent by taking a course in drawing, which meant that he would have to move to the city. He put forth his plans to his parents, but his proposal was met with rejection. His parents were terrified. They were afraid about how their child would survive in a city full of maniacs. But Avinash didn't agree. He told them that he wasn't going to make any compromises this time.

When he broke the tradition by deciding to move to the city, he faced enormous pressure from the people in the village. But he withstood all the opposition because he believed he was doing the right thing. Besides, when his family appealed to the head of the panchayat, he supported Avinash's decision by saying that young talent like him should go out and explore the world. He also promised him some monetary help. Although his parents were hurt by the fact that he had gone against their wishes, Avinash thought he would pacify them by finding some fancy job and sending them money. But nothing in this world came without a price.

When he moved to the city of his dreams, Bangalore, a long list of obstacles awaited him. With no proper degree and a vague picture of what he wanted to do in his life, he discovered that finding a decent job was as difficult as doing nothing. Soon, he ran out of the money the village panchayat had given him. The fear of failure, and apprehension of not realizing his dreams haunted him day and night. In desperation, he took up whatever job he could, no matter how menial. He worked as a manual labourer, a petrol station attendant, a server in a restaurant, and even painted hoardings and theatrical backdrops.

Right from his childhood days, Avinash had never been able to resist the lure of colour, form and texture, and he would draw willingly and passionately whenever he found the time. He would spend his day sitting under a tree, sketching. Now all those early, scratchy strokes could be transformed into professional drawings, he decided, when he finally joined in one of the finest arts colleges in Bangalore with whatever little money he had saved. After a struggle of two years, the satisfaction he felt was unlike anything he had known before. To ease his financial burden, he also worked as a part-time librarian in the same college currently.

Now, the bike took a left turn to the main road leading to the railway station. Avinash saw the roads were slowly coming alive, unlike in his area. The locals had already started their day, although there were still some homeless people sleeping on the pavement. He whizzed past roadside vendors selling coffee and snacks. He felt the urge to take a two-minute break to sip a steaming cup of coffee, which he thought would ease the icy numbness in his body. But he resisted and sped away. And there was a reason behind it. He wanted to share the joy of sipping coffee with his childhood friend Sahas, whose train would be arriving in a few minutes. He had been anticipating such a moment for a long time.

Sahas and Avinash had grown up together in the same hilly village of Agumbe and their friendship went back to the days when they wore shorts and carried heavy school bags. They had forged a very special bond from the moment they met and had been inseparable friends since then. Avinash clearly remembered the day when they had first met, although it was not a happy occasion. He was ten years old then and had gone with a group of friends to hang out near the cascading waterfalls. Suddenly, he heard someone screaming out that a kid from their group was drowning in the pond. Avinash didn't know at that time it was Sahas who was bobbing in and out of the water, thrashing his arms and calling out for help. Some boys stood around helplessly as some ran off to get the help of villagers. Avinash didn't know what exactly had made him to act so bravely that day, but he quickly pulled off his shirt, dove into the water and swam towards Sahas, tossing him the shirt. Sahas had held on to his shirt and was safely pulled to the shore. After a stressful three minutes of trying to resuscitate him, Sahas had regained consciousness and started coughing out water. Avinash had never forgotten his pale and frightened face when he had opened eyes and recalled his terrible experience. Since then, Sahas had followed Avinash silently, no matter where he went in the village. They strolled through the dense forest, pausing now and then to admire the flora and fauna. Sometimes, he would sit beside Avinash silently, looking at his drawings admiringly. After school, he would take Avinash to his mother's hotel and feed him her delicious tatte idlis.

Avinash pulled up the bike beside a snack vendor outside the railway station and dashed inside. Shouldering the passengers rushing here and there and vendors crying out "chai-chai," "idli-wada", he raked his eager eyes through the crowd to catch a glimpse of his friend. But he couldn't find Sahas anywhere. There was an empty train standing on the platform, the one Sahas should have come by. It meant he was already here.

Avinash got a bit worried because his friend wasn't used to the city like he was. He couldn't even catch a bus on his own and would panic for little things. But soon Avinash's face stretched to a wide grin when he finally spotted him.

Sahas sat on a small bench looking like an innocent, lost puppy, next to a man puffing a cigarette and staring around clueless.

Avinash clamped a hand over the mouth to stifle the laugh exploding out of his mouth at reading his friend's face: Did I really get onto the train I was supposed to? Why isn't my friend here? Where am I supposed to go now?

For a moment, Avinash had the urge to hide somewhere behind the wall and watch that face, but he couldn't, for he knew his friend.

"Hey Sahas," he exclaimed, running towards his friend. But before he was enveloped in to a hug, Sahas threw his bag at him with an angry face.

"I've been waiting here for the last half an hour. Where the hell were you man? People have been looking at me as if I were a chain-snatcher. I've been so worried," he said, almost in a crying tone.

Avinash picked up his bag from the ground and dusted it off. "Cool down, buddy, your train is a little early. Besides, you haven't come to the Amazon forests, okay. This is Bangalore," he grinned.

"That would have been much better. At lease the forest would be like our village," Sahas murmured.

Avinash shook his head and gave him a hard hug, much against his will, which wasn't new to both. "Thanks for coming man. You have no idea how long I have been waiting for this day." Sahas smiled, all the worry vanishing away.

"You know what?" Avinash went on to make his friend feel better as they walked. "When I first moved to this city, I was lost. I was making rounds and hadn't even realized it was a big park. You won't believe it, but it took me almost two hours to walk out from there. And when I hit the streets, the noise of vehicles, traffic, hullaballoo of auto-walas, was so different from our village environment. They made me so anxious that I wanted to run back home," he laughed. "You're very lucky to have someone pick you up from the station!"

Soon, they headed towards Avinash's room. En route, they stopped at a coffee stall. Holding the warm tumblers around their palms and sipping the freshly-brewed piping hot coffee, they reminisced about their childhood. Those had been the best days of their life.

Suddenly, Bangalore looked more beautiful than it had ever to Avinash before. He wished his friend would stay with him forever like this. But fate sometimes had its own plans. And now, it was all set to poke its lazy finger into their innocent friendship, which was going to change forever. Both the friends were too engrossed, laughing and chatting, too blind to foresee what was about to happen.

When his friend unlocked the room door, Sahas stood outside, wearing a familiar, frowning look on his face at the sight of the room. A variety of art materials lay strewn across the floor, covered in layers of dust. There didn't seem to be any space for them to even enter.

Avinash threw a sheepish grin and walked inside, picking things up. "You know, I got back late from work last night and then overslept, so I couldn't clean my room," he said, apologizing for the untidiness.

Sahas smiled. They both knew that Avinash had never bothered to tidy up his house back in the village either. Sahas recalled how his friend's mother would run behind him with a broomstick after finding a heap of pencil shavings in the cooking pot. Now, he had no one to supervise him. But this did not bother Sahas. He loved his friend, no matter what he was or did.

"Maybe all creative people have messy rooms," Sahas pointed out.

"Only you will say that!" Avinash said, recalling how Sahas had always backed his every action. They both exchanged warm glances. "I'm so happy you're here. I wish you had come here a long time ago," he said, his eyes spilling warmth. When he had come to Bangalore two years ago, he had tried to persuade Sahas to join him. But his friend had refused because of his mother.

Sahas had been brought up by his mother, a single parent. She ran a small hotel in their village for the many tourists who came to Agumbe. It was a very basic hotel with few amenities or zero luxuries. Yet tourists and locals would flock there to relish her flavoursome dishes, particularly her special tatte idli, which she would garnish with special spices and cook over a fire of twigs in a traditional way. She had struggled very hard to educate him. When she asked her son to join his friend in Bangalore to pursue his education, Sahas had obstinately refused. He had told her clearly that he wasn't going to leave her. She was disappointed by his decision, because like every mother, she wanted her son to flourish in his career. She knew that if he stayed in the village, he would just end up as the best server in their hotel. And she didn't want that for him. So she had coaxed Sahas until he had accepted her wish, despite the anguish of her son's departure. She knew that he was a strong, sincere and bright student who deserved a promising future.

"So, how do you like the room?" Avinash enquired.

Before Sahas could open his mouth, Avinash walked into the kitchen. "Yeah, I know you'll love it. In fact, it's the best," he shouted from there. "I'm placing the tiffin on the plate – idli and wada. They may not taste like Mum's tatte idli, but they're not that bad either," he said serving the breakfast they had brought on their way home.

"Look at my drawings. There's a catalogue lying beside the heap of clothes, which has my latest ones," he went on, hoping his friend wouldn't be bored. But he still didn't hear Sahas. A moment later, Avinash emerged from the kitchen with a tray of steaming hot coffee and plates filled with breakfast, imagining Sahas flipping through his drawings, filled with admiration.

But Sahas was doing nothing like that. He stood by the grubby window staring at the open ground, opposite the house where some boys were playing football.

Avinash placed the tray down on the bed and walked up to his silent friend. "What are you up to?" he said from behind. When Sahas spun around, he gathered that something was wrong.

Sahas looked homesick and sad. His eyes clearly conveyed how much he was missing his mother. After living together for so many years, this was the first time he was away from her.

Avinash threw his arm around him to comfort him. "Trust me, she'll fine," he assured. "I know how emotionally attached you are to her and the village. But believe me, whenever you move to a new place and no matter what hurdles you face, the place will embrace you. Do you know that the first thing I noticed on the streets of Bangalore when I lost my way? It was the beautiful wall paintings, the one that gave me an insight into the city's culture? They also gave me hope that artists like me would survive." He smiled at the memory, recalling his first day in Bangalore. "So, I am sure though you're a little down now, things will get better once you start your college."

"Would you like to see my latest drawings?" he added excitedly, secretly wishing to distract his friend's glum mood.

Sahas nodded his head silently.

Avinash quickly fetched the large portfolio with his latest drawings. They both sat down on the bed with the drawings spread in front of them.

Sahas's empty eyes were instantly replaced with delight as he looked at them. Many of them were of women. He knew his friend was an expert at portraying the live beauty of women – their large provocative eyes, their tempting pomegranate lips and their curvaceous bodies. But it wasn't just their beauty; some drawings conveyed the unflinching grit of women on battlefields too. According to Avinash, every woman is born with a unique beauty, be it the curve of her body or fiery eyes; someone had to discover that or possess eyes like his to see the real beauty behind the outward façade.

"This one looks as if you were held at gunpoint when you drew it," Sahas teased, tapping on a drawing of a woman whose eyes looked distorted before pushing it over to Avinash.

"Yes, it was indeed," he said, inspecting. "The lady was in a rush and she had lots of specifications besides. You see, for an artist, freedom is the best tool.,"

Sahas nodded.

Gradually their conversation slipped into the past. On how Avinash during their schooldays would sit for hours on the last bench, his eyes glued on the drawing he was making. When the drawing was finished, it used to be circulated around the whole class so that his friends could scribble comments below it. In fact, Sahas was always the first to see and comment on it.

Remembering and recalling the past eased Sahas's anxiety a little. When Avinash sensed that his friend would be fine on his own, he bid him goodbye and left for work. Before leaving, he lent him his mobile so that Sahas could call his mom. His friend didn't own a mobile in those days.

After his friend left, Sahas made a call to the paid phone booth in his village. In those days, having a mobile in villages was considered as big a privilege as owing a Benz. The boy from the phone booth ran to his mom's hotel, which was a few kilometres away, to give her the message. On receiving the message, his mom would have to walk all the way to the phone booth to receive her son's call. And in return, she would be charged for the call according to the time she spent on the phone. Things weren't that easy in those days.

Meanwhile, waiting for his mom to arrive at the phone booth, Sahas stared out of the window, endless thoughts running in his head. He was only here to fulfill his mother's wish: to pursue his education in one of the best colleges. But he never wanted to come here, never ever! And it wasn't just leaving his mother; something else had been bothering him from the time he stepped into this city. This place reminded him of his secret, the one with which he lived all his life, the one he'd never ever shared with anyone, not even with his best friend Avinash. The eager anticipation that Sahas would study well and earn was soon replaced by an unknown fear and worry and he felt like instantly running away. No matter how much he tried to push away this niggling discomfort, he couldn't help but wonder what would happen if his worst nightmare came true.

At once, Sahas felt so weak and helpless, like someone had punched him hard.

It was 7.00 p.m. Avinash put his pencil down on the table and flexed his muscles, looking around. There was no one in the library. As the librarian in the Arts College, he was usually very busy throughout the day, checking books in and out, supervising the students and arranging the books in their allotted places. But unlike most afternoons, there was no rush today. It was too late for anyone to stay in the college this time. Normally he would have left by now, but having skipped a few hours in the morning to bring his friend from the station, he had adjusted the time by working late. With nothing to do, he buried himself in his drawings, his best pastime, though his heart wanted to be with his friend whom he was meeting after so many years.

He put the finished drawing into his portfolio and shoved it into his bag. He then entered his exit time in the register, locked the library and handed over the keys to the dean, whose room was two blocks away.

When Avinash walked out, it was dark. Even though it was only 7.00 p.m., the sky dazzled with stars as if it was midnight. The college seemed abandoned, almost like a haunted place.

It was actually located far away from the heart of the city, so there wasn't much hue and cry even during peak hours. Avinash hopped on his bike and headed down to the nearby bus stop. He pulled his bike by the public telephone booth for a moment to make a call to Sahas about their dinner plans. Avinash wanted to take him out for a nice dinner. He wasn't a good cook and always filled his tummy with instant noodles. But he didn't want to frighten his friend with his culinary skills today, not on the first day at least. Besides, a small new Chinese restaurant had opened a few kilometres away from his room and he had heard very good reviews about the food.

He dropped a coin into the call box and dialled his own number, looking around. The bus stop was eerily empty, except for a girl who was standing a few steps away from him, probably waiting for her bus. He couldn't see her face as she had her back to him. The phone beeped thrice and the coin slipped down into the open rectangular space. Perhaps, the call didn't get connected. He collected the coin and dropped it again into the box, his eyes lingering on the girl standing there.

God, she had such long black hair that had been tied in a single braid. Avinash had never been an admirer of long hair. He felt girls looked cuter in shoulder length hair that bobbed up and down when they talked or laughed. And undoubtedly, Bangalore was filled with so many cute, short-haired girls. But what he was looking at today was different. The shiny braid with unruly curls at the end looked stunning, so natural. It was like a long black snake had slithered out of a forest and attached itself to the girl's back. And besides, who said watching long hair was boring? Avinash's eyes were glued to her hair. He was so hypnotized that he forgot the world around him, even the sound of his mobile ringing in his ears. The only thing he wished for in that moment was to have a pencil in his hand rather than a telephone to depict her beauty.

"Hello, hello..." Sahas shouted on the phone again.

"H... Hi, I am sorry Sahas. I didn't, didn't hear... you," Avinash stuttered, his eyes still on her hair.

"Even our neighbors can hear my yells. Where are you?"

Avinash came to his senses. "I am still at college; we'll have dinner..." his voice trailed off when the girl turned around to glance at him, as if sensing a stranger was watching her. "Shit, I think she just caught me staring at her."

"Who caught you?" Just then, a bunch of guys who didn't look like students pulled up their bikes at the bus stop, laughing. They looked like louts in their mismatched clothes with scarves wrapped around their necks. They were talking among themselves loudly, laughing their ass out at their own jokes and whistling. Oh yes, whistling at the girl!

Sensing that they were more dangerous than a stranger watching her, the girl walked a few steps away from them cautiously. And so did they!

"I called you... I called you for... I think she's in trouble," Avinash faltered again. He couldn't recall why he had made the call. His eyes were glued on the guys taunting the girl. Although he couldn't hear them clearly, he sensed something suspicious.

"Who's in trouble? Avi, are you okay?" Sahas's voice faded away. It was only their taunts Avinash could hear.

"Man, she's damn beautiful," one guy remarked wickedly from the gang.

The girl stood with folded arms, defiantly looking away from them.

"Don't you think it will be fun to ride on her?" another guy suggested.

The girl threw a fierce 'fuck off' look at them, but it didn't seem to help.

"How about the payment then?" one more guy chirped in, throwing his arm recklessly on his friend's shoulder.

"I don't think she would even exceed thousand bucks." They all laughed out loudly.

Avinash was still holding onto the telephone, but his entire attention was on the guys.

"Avi, I really don't know if you can hear me or not, but the dinner is ready, okay? Come home quickly," Sahas literally yelled down the phone and hung up, wondering what was wrong with his friend's brain.

"Okay, I'll call you later," said Avinash to the disconnected beep sound, not even realizing that his friend had hung up.

He quickly marched towards the guys who were still passing awful comments to the girl. As he approached, he could faintly hear them talking about some room and payment. And he wasn't an innocent to size up what the hell they were talking about. His blood boiled and his face went hot. She may be a stranger to him, but she was a girl in need. It had become a common joke to target a lone woman these days, he thought heatedly, taking huge strides towards them. It looked like he would knock the bunch of them down in one fell swoop, just like in the movies. He stood in front of them with clenched fists, staring angrily at them. But the guys weren't bothered and continued to tease the girl.

"What are you doing here?" Avinash suddenly turned towards the girl.

The girl looked at him shocked.

The guys fell utterly silent. A shade of panic caught them, wondering if they both knew each other.

"What the hell are you doing here?" Avinash was glaring at the girl. "Now, enough is enough. Are you getting on the bike or should I talk to your parents?"

The girl glared back at him puzzled. She didn't even know him, nor had she seen him before. Here was a complete stranger asking her to sit on his bike. But there weren't any mental hospitals nearby either to assume he had escaped from there.

"How many times will you fight with me? See, I have no patience left. Let's go talk to your parents and finalize the divorce," Avinash looked away from her defiantly. Of course, he could try his hand at acting as well, apart from drawing. He knew he was a fucking genius.

The girl's mouth fell open in shock. Anything the size of a huge frog could easily have hopped into it.

"If you're not coming with me right now, I swear I'll knock your teeth down your throat," he said, glaring at the boys with a furious frown, clearly implying that the punch line was for them and not for the girl. The next minute, they hopped onto their bikes and swooped down the street disappearing, assuming the worst. The girl heaved a sigh but didn't look very gratified to be called his wife. She looked seriously at Avinash with her large eyes.

But who wanted to look at those hazelnut eyes when the long shiny braid danced behind her. Avinash scrunched his nose in mild embarrassment. "I am sorry for that. But I didn't want to end up in a street fight, you know,' he made it sound so casual. "Not that I'm bad at fighting, you know, we have been trained with basic moves in our school to even fight back a bunch," he started to kick his arms and knees in to the empty air trying to flaunt his skills chorusing 'oohh, aahh'.

Ok, he had to stop now. The girl was looking at him like he was a goon trying to trap her with his antics. "Where do you want to go, by the way?" he resumed standing, trying to sound friendly. "I can drop you if you could tell the place."

The girl was still looking at him suspiciously. "Thanks, but the bus is just about to come now," she glanced at her watch. Her recent experience had made her wary of all guys.

"But, I don't think there are any buses right now along this route," he shrugged confidently like he had been travelling around this time frequently by buses. The fact was he was hinting that she'd fall into trouble again if she didn't take his help.

But the next moment, he had to bite his tongue when a bus pulled up at the stop from nowhere. Damn! Was she working with the transportation department or was her father a conductor?

The girl glanced at him as Avinash made himself busy darting his eyes furiously in an attempt to avoid her gaze.

She walked slowly and paused before passing him. "Thanks," she murmured, looking at him from the corner of her eyes and went towards the bus. Her long shiny hair danced behind her bum as she leapt inside.

"You're welcome."Avinash said in a very low voice to the departing girl. He didn't even know if she heard him or not. He just stood there, watching her and the long hair, wondering if he would ever meet her again. He didn't know where she lived or even her name. Yet, he badly wanted to know more about her, though he knew, it was too late for that.

The girl sat beside the window and threw a last goodbye look at him. And then she smiled, probably a genuine smile for his saving her from the goons, or perhaps she thought it was the last time she was going to see him. They were two complete strangers who had met by accident. But life sometimes throws you such encounters only to leave behind indelible memories.

The conductor blew the whistle.

Avinash still stood there, watching the girl, not able to stop the desire to know more about her. But he didn't have the slightest clue that since destiny had planned this meeting, there would be no more coincidences.

Soon, the bus whizzed past him. Avinash had never loved long hair so madly until recently.

"I'm sorry man, I'm late. Let's go out for dinn—" Avinash's words hung in the air, his jaw dropping down in awe when Sahas opened the door to his room.

"Welcome home, sir. What are you holding up to?"

His room, his pig room looked completely different from what it was when Avinash had left for work. All the clothes, drawing accessories and papers were off the floor and had been well organized in separate shelves without him racking his brain to reach out for anything. There wasn't a single speck of dust anywhere. As he walked into the kitchen, he noticed it looked as tidy and spotless as the living room. Avinash had always complained that he had rented the smallest room ever.

But today, his house looked pretty large, large enough to sprawl across the floor all through the night without clothes. He could easily guess whose hand went in for such a ship-shape room.

"You did this all?" he looked at Sahas with gratitude. He could imagine how his friend had scrubbed all those tiles, grubby windows, and dust-laden fans and tidied up every nook and corner.

Sahas simply shrugged like it wasn't a big deal. "The dinner is ready too. I told you on the phone, but you seemed to be living in another planet when I was talking to you. What had gotten into you, by the way?"

The memory of that long-haired girl came back in bits and pieces to Avinash and the hair on his neck stood stiff. Damn, what was happening to him? "Oh man! That's a long story, I'll tell you later. Now the mice have started to race around in my tummy. Let's have dinner."

By the time Avinash emerged, freshened up, Sahas had arranged the dinner on the tiny terrace waiting for his friend, yet again giving him another jolt of surprise. Dinner on the terrace, Avinash thought excitingly, rubbing his hands together. How long had it been he sat idly, enjoying the supper. He counted on the blessings for sending his friend to him. They both sat under the open sky dazzling with stars with the moon showering its silvery glow. The scent of freshly made food lifted their spirits. Sahas had made peppery rice and dal to accompany the homemade appam his mother had sent, and the melting sweet kesari bath he kept aside for dessert peeped yummily from a steel bowl. Avinash took a hot, sloppy morsel of rice and dal topped with crunchy appam into his mouth and his face was a worth to watch.

He got surrendered to its delectable taste: tangy, mildly sweet, and spicy, and above all, the taste of homemade food that he got to taste after many years.

"Mmm… this tastes like heaven and home after so many years," he said, his mouth dripping with dal, fully relishing the magic of his friend's hand. Sahas grinned, his tummy almost filled at his friend's expression.

As the night progressed, they talked, laughed and reminisced about the old days over the delicious meal, celebrating being together once again.

It was a sunny Monday morning. After having spent a whole week with his friend around Bangalore lanes in the evenings, Sahas now stood in front of the college with the admission receipt in his hand, a small bag behind his back with the supply of books and a tense, excited look in his eyes. Mount Victoria College was sprawled across a huge campus, filled with lots and lots of trees, a sign of the authorities' green thumb. It was one of the city's most prestigious colleges where students yearn to get a seat. When Sahas got admission into the college to study accounts, he was ecstatic. It was a subject that would inject a dose of business awareness into the running of his village hotel. He was on top of the world and so was his mother. No wonder, as it was arguably one of the hardest colleges to get into. Though he found it difficult to stay away from his beloved mother, he had always secretly dreamed of joining such an elite college. Now his secret wish had come true. He could soon help his mother to make their own tiny hotel turn in to a big one, and who knew, maybe they could open a chain of hotels. He'd read stories about such people who started with nothing and then went on to build an empire. God, he could almost picture his mother's beaming face at her son's achievements.

He headed straight to the Accounts block, located exactly three rooms before the office. By now, he was well acquainted with every nook and cranny of the campus as he had explored it with his friend over the weekend. As he walked, he could see students thronging everywhere. Some were new like him, with the application forms in their hands and immense rapture in their eyes. And some were seniors. They were sitting on the huge windowsills along the corridor, informally meeting the freshers, ragging the new students. When Sahas hurried past them, his head hung low. He was stopped by a bunch of seniors. He felt moisture under his arms, feeling nervy, fearing what was to come. He was no good at dealing with social monsters.

A senior from the group demanded that he demonstrate his muscle fat, like in weightlifting. The task given to him was nothing when compared to fellow freshers where few students were made to sit topless in a frog position. Probably, they sensed he was the fragile boy from a village and gave him a comparatively easy task. But Sahas felt so terrified, the hand clutching the form tightened in grip. He helplessly stood rooted in his place. The seniors who were shooting disapproving glances at his panicky face had no clue how shy he was.

"Come on man, just show your muscles and leave. What's the big deal?" a senior shouted at him.

This made Sahas even more terrified. He closed his eyes and tried to recall what Avinash had said the previous night. He had advised him not to look feeble, especially in front of the seniors who prey on the weak. That moment Sahas wished for a scrape of courage his friend had.

The senior called another boy, probably a fresher, and asked him to show his muscles. The guy did it in a jiffy and left. Sahas simply stood there, shy and abashed, unable to overcome his fear of social situations. The tears were minutes away. Before the seniors got irritated with his silence, one of them called a girl who was walking past them. Luckily, the entire focus was shifted to her.

When the girl walked towards them, there were whispers among them on how cute and innocent she looked. Despite the fear, Sahas couldn't help but raise his head and quickly steal a glance at her. Yeah, she was indeed cute. But she also looked lost and confused just like him. Who wants to rag a shy village boy when a beautiful junior is around? Sahas thought. "Why do you look so confused?" a senior asked her.

"Sir, I'm looking for the economics block. I'm new to the college and I couldn't find it anywhere," the girl said in a voice which was softer than melted butter.

"Fresher?"

"Yes sir!"

"Walk two classes straight, take a right turn, cross the bushy path and wait there," the senior said almost in a commanding voice. His friends started to giggle as the girl left following his instructions. The other juniors looked at her gob-smacked, wondering how she had been let off so easily. While all this was going on, someone shouted that the dean was on his, checking rounds. The next moment, seniors dispersed hastily and the juniors left for their respective classes.

Sahas heaved a sigh of relief, thanking god under his breath. He took his bag and wore it on his back. He then slowly walked in the direction of his class with the girl who had just asked for directions ahead of him. His instincts said he had to stop the girl for a minute and say something. Though he hesitated initially, he finally worked up some courage and stopped her. "Excuse me."

At first, the girl didn't seem to hear him as she kept walking. Although he said to himself to let go of her, his inner voice made him call the girl again. "Excuse me," Sahas said a little louder.

The girl swivelled around. "Did you just call me?"

He silently nodded his head.

"What is it about?"

"I'm sorry but I'm afraid that the directions you were given by the seniors were wrong,"

"Oh really?" she made a doubtful face. "Why would you say that?"

It's because they're morons, he wanted to say but simply shrugged. "I just know it."

The girl looked at him suspiciously. "Who are you, by the way?"

"I'm a fresher and this is my first day."

"Oh!" She sighed, wondering why the seniors who were well acquainted with the college map would give her wrong directions. And then something dawned upon her. Damn, it had not been even an hour that she had walked into the college and the guy was already on his way flirting with her. What a daft, she thought irritatingly. "Disgusting fellow, didn't you find anyone to flirt with? You idiot!" She walked away throwing him a fishy look, muttering under her breath.

Sahas, who was too stupid to even understand why the girl had walked away without responding, scratched his head in confusion. He was only trying to help her. He shook his head and went back to his own block. Avinash was indeed right when he would joke that his friend's brain was probably half-eaten by bugs during his sleep!

The girl, on the other hand, as per the directions given by the seniors took the other side. But later, she had to bite her tongue in embarrassment when she found herself standing right in front of the gents' toilet. "Economics block is right inside," one from a bunch of guys who were eagerly awaiting her arrival teased, pointing his finger in the line of toilets. They were all giggling, hissing and laughing. Resisting the urge to slap them on their faces, she quickly walked back, not wanting to spoil her first day. After marching to the other side furiously, she spotted Sahas ahead of her, who was slowly making his way towards his block.

"Hey," she stopped him as Sahas turned around. She walked up to him. "I'm sorry. I didn't know you were trying to help me," she said with an apologetic look.

Sahas gave a shy smile and shrugged like it was okay.

"Hi, I'm Aarti," she extended a confident hand for a friendly shake, wanting to clear the earlier misunderstanding.

Sahas hesitantly reached out for her hand. He felt too embarrassed to even do it as though he was hugging a girl in public. Befriending girls was a tougher task than flying a plane for him. The only woman he had ever been close to was his mother.

"The Economics block is just beside the Accounts. Come, I'll show you," he said and they both walked together.

"So which block do you belong to?" the girl asked.

"Accounts." he said and after a moment of silence, he countered, "So, where are you from?"

They talked until they reached their respective blocks. The girl thanked him again and left for her class.

Sahas stepped inside his own cheerful class, full of freshers. His heart at first chugged at the speed of a fast-moving train glancing at a large group of perky, young girls and boys who looked at their best in posh clothes and lively nature. Many questions poked around his head: Would I fit into the group? Would I be able to overcome the fear of mingling with people? Would I be able to study hard and make my mom happy? Etc... etc... Endless questions went on and on inside his head, making him panic. But then the dream of seeing his mother happy forever and the aspiration of wanting to ace in such an elite, prestigious college made him move forward. He sat on the second row seat, waiting for the class to begin, a new beginning to the path of his success.

Sometimes in life, some incidents are too mysterious to just be a coincidence. And when there are many such coincidences, fate will certainly play a role. Indeed, there are millions of people in this world, but when you meet a particular person over and over again, it means that fate is trying to put something in your path. Now, is it for the good or bad, let's leave it to fate...

On the same Monday morning, people in the city were bidding goodbye to a restful weekend and were going about their routines in a similar fizzy manner. The bus stand near Wilson Road was a perfect example of it. It was teeming with people waiting for their buses to their respective colleges and offices. In the crowd was Avinash standing with his cross bag slung across his shoulder, rolls of paper peeping out from the top of it. He was on his way to his usual work. He usually rode the bike to the library, but having given it for servicing, he opted for a regular bus today. Soon, the bus pulled up at the stop. People thronged, elbowing each other, pushing their way inside. They stood like tightly packed sardines in a can. Avinash leapt inside with great difficulty and managed to stand on the foot board. It was like warfare. Regular habit of travelling by bike had made it difficult for him to manage the crowd, but he knew it was just a matter of minutes, because most of the commuters were probably Loyala students who would get off at the next stop.

As he struggled to hang out from the crowd amidst the squeezed, tight bodies, Avinash's eyes suddenly twinkled at something. Something that looked very familiar and delightful as though he could never forget it for his lifetime. At first, he ignored, assuming he was day dreaming. But when he came upon the image again, his body stood erected with attention, eyes seeking for the girl. The same girl with the shiny long braid, the one he had helped a couple of days earlier at his college. It appeared like the girl stood in the middle of an aisle between seating areas among other women. At once, he had a hazy rewind of that cold night when the girl had thanked him, their brief conversation, with her smiling from behind the glass window. Avinash's heart skipped a beat. Before he lost the girl from his eye sight, he swept his gaze back to the crowd and began searching for her to make sure he wasn't day dreaming. But hanging down from a moving bus and searching for a girl, especially for her hair, wasn't that easy. All he could see were ladies' bums: M, L, X, XXL, varied sizes. God, if someone caught him staring at the ladies' bums; they'd collectively push him out from the bus or stone him to death with their ragged tickets. His thoughts halted when the bus pulled at the Loyola College. Large number of students hastily got off the bus as expected and headed towards their college entry gate, chatting and laughing. Avinash, who was still hoping to catch a glimpse of the long-haired miracle, furiously ran his eyes at the student group. But he couldn't spot her. He then looked around the half-empty bus, just in case she was inside. But she wasn't there either. His face sank in disappointment. So, he was indeed daydreaming all this time. He couldn't quite get over the obsession to see the girl once again. Shit, what is happening to me, he thought.

The conductor blew the whistle and the driver cranked up the engine. Just then, the miracle happened. No, he wasn't day dreaming. There she was, standing close to the driver seat, holding the bar and giving way to the crowd. Perhaps the large frame ahead the first seat might have shielded her. Avinash's eyes, at once, took the shape of a large rainbow. His heart was beating as wildly as a church bell. It was so exciting and delightful to bump into her. He wondered why he was being flooded with overwhelming emotions and though he sounded stupid to even himself, he couldn't help his joy. There was indeed something about this mysterious girl that drove him crazy.

The girl slid into a vacant seat by the window and was absently twirling the front locks of her hair, staring out. Avinash stood two seats behind her, quickly rehearsing what to say to her. He'd casually say hi, thank her, sorry why should he thank her? Or perhaps take thanks from her, ask her name, what she does, blah,

blah…and then leave. It sounded as simple as it looked, but his legs trembled. Oh god, why was he so terrified? Even the seat next to her was vacant. See, even god wanted to help him. For a moment, he debated whether to sit beside her or casually talk with one hand gripping a hanging strap, him leaning forward. But fear loomed in. What if the girl didn't recognize him, or worse, looked at him as though he was a moron who had sat beside a girl without her permission?

Ok, why was he planning too much? It wasn't as though he was about to act in a play. Ok, enough of loitering. Simply go and say hi before she gets off the bus, he decided. When he was about to go, a lady in her forties excused him and said she wanted to perch on the seat and that he was blocking her way. God, her hand was pointing at his girl. Sorry, the girl. Avinash quickly came back to earth. "Would you mind sitting over there?" he asked her politely, pointing to a vacant seat in another row.

The lady threw him a suspicious look.

"Oh, actually," he lowered his voice, "that's my wife sitting over there. We had a petty fight this morning about breakfast. I wanted to have wada and she wanted to make her trademark idli. And then we fought. I still wonder how Idli and wada in hotels make an inseparable combination." He sighed theoretically. "So I wanted to have a little chat with her and settle down the dispute. Hope you don't mind." The lady took a long, suspicious look at him and then nodded her head briefly before walking to the other row saying, "No problem!"

Avinash's heart was filled with a strange pride at how easily he had convinced the lady. But he should make an important note that women these days were throwing suspicious looks at him very often. He hastily raked his tousled hair which had got dishevelled in the crowd. Gathering all the courage, he marched past the girl's seat nonchalantly at first and then turned around, surprise registering on his face. "Hi," he said dropping down next to her casually. He tried to sound as gob-smacked as possible as though he was spotting her for the first time. "So good to see you here." He gave his trademark, charming smile. The girl snapped her head around. Her face registered no surprise unlike his fake one and thankfully no suspicions either. She recognized him immediately, but had never assumed he'd land up right next to her like this, out of the blue. "Oh hi!" she said a little hesitantly. "What are you doing here?"

"So have you recognized me?" he asked her, his eyes full of anxiety like he hadn't heard her.

The girl nodded her head as if to imply, yes I did and that's why I said 'hi' followed by 'what are you doing here?' dammit! She had no clue the excitement of seeing her made him slightly deaf.

"You know, I was thinking about you the other day. I meant that day when you were in trouble. I had been worrying since then if you had reached home safely… " Ok, he needed to stop to breathe. Also, slow down a little, coz, the girl was looking at him a little awkwardly. Slow and steady wins the race.

"Are you stalking me?" she suddenly cut him off.

Avinash couldn't help a round of coughing pit followed with tears swell in his eyes. Shit. "Wh… what?" he stuttered, shifting uncomfortably in his seat. "Why would you say that? I mean, do I look like that?" he asked, a little shamed. So much for thinking the girl hadn't registered any suspicion. Stalking?

"Well then, you should know something. The cool opening line when you spot a stranger is 'I think I know her' or 'she's my friend'." The girl paused and looked at him knowingly, "but not Idli and wada dispute, and whatever made you say that?" she flicked her finger at the woman who was sitting in the next row.

Avinash's heart slipped down to his stomach. "Oh shit," he mumbled under his breath with utter shame. So she had heard his entire bullshit story. That moment he wished the bus would suddenly break down or crash into some pole with no injuries to the passengers. At least such a mishap would take the girl's mind off what he had just said. The girl continued to look at him accusingly with her big fierce eyes. If she had a knife in her tender hands, it would surely end up on his throat.

"I'm sorry, please don't get me wrong," he gathered up some nerve. "It's just…" he thought at length on what to say, knowing nothing could back up his bloody story, "It's just that I'm an outgoing guy," he said at last, hating his own back up theory.

The girl looked at him unconvinced apparently, anger pouring out of her eyes. "Aha, I don't think this is the first ever time you mentioned that. Do you recall the night we met at the bus stand?" she had him recall.

Now this wasn't going the way he had assumed. He took a quick gulp of fresh air. The girl was shooting death glares at him. "Okay, I'm sorry." his eyes resumed honesty. "Actually I saw you when I first got into the bus, but wasn't sure if it was you. And then I searched you among the students, still you weren't there. But when I spotted you again," he paused, the twinkle dazzling in his eyes, "I kind of felt happy… a little happy, nope, very happy indeed." He looked into her eyes. He could see she was attentive, if not flattered. "So finally I decided I would say a proper hi, because I wasn't sure if I'd meet you again. But then I was afraid that the lady with her fiery, silver curls, who is still watching us from her seat with her hazel nut eyes, would spoil everything. So..." he shrugged, not daring to finish his obvious, make up story.

The girl said nothing for a long time. Suddenly she found her bag interesting, which she kept zipping and unzipping. An embarrassing silence hung in between them for a moment. But good thing, she didn't look furious.

"Okay." She nodded her head, after which the silence felt like ages. Actually, she even looked a little impressed by his blunt frankness accompanied by an award winning speech on how he encountered her.

Honesty could always splash its magic on girls. Taking advantage of that look on her face, he quickly added, "If you're not comfortable with me sitting beside you, I'll leave right away." He slowly lifted his body off the seat unwillingly, hoping she'd stop him.

"It's okay, I'm fine," the girl said.

Avinash breathed a sigh of relief and did a little zumba dance inside. He knew he was a genius in dealing with girls. "Thanks." He smiled as they both exchanged few awkward glances. There was a taut silence before the girl spoke.

"So, what is it about the way you look at people?"

He looked at her like he quiet didn't get her.

"I mean, the way you just described the lady. Fiery, silver curls, hazel nut eyes..." she mimicked him, snapping her eyes at the lady who was still watching them to see if they made up their quarrel or not about the breakfast. "Are you a writer or something?"

Avinash looked at her puzzled, flipping his eyes between the lady and then back at the girl. Out of all the fabulous, award-winning speech he had just made, she had only picked the description of the lady? Was she really ok?

"I'm sorry, but I really quiet didn't get what you meant?" he said.

Just then, conductor came and interrupted their conversation, asking for a ticket. Avinash reached into his pockets and pulled the balled ticket and showed. The girl reached for her bag and pulled out her monthly pass. So, she regularly commutes through this way, probably in the same bus, he quickly made a mental note.

Once the conductor was out of earshot, the girl spoke again.

"I mean, you stare at people a lot, don't you?" she said, putting away her pass in to the hand bag. "Especially women, right? Don't you lie now, okay."

"Yes, I do watch people," Avinash shrugged nonchalantly, "what's so offensive about it?"

"Nothing offensive, but it kind of makes people a little uncomfortable, you see."

"You have a point," he nodded, "but without looking at people, how could I do my job?"

"What's your job? Watching people and then weaving an idli-wada story?" she teased.

"No, my job is to mirror their moments on a piece of paper. You see, I'm an artist, I draw them. So I watch them," he said as a matter of fact.

The girl stopped fiddling with her bag and snapped her head up, caught by surprise. Avinash could clearly see the awe of admiration flowing from her eyes. It was such a delight to watch people's reaction when he said he was an artist.

For a moment, she was lost in her own thoughts. "Show me your pass, quick madam." The conductor's sharp, impatient voice ahead of them to one of the commuters, tapping the ticket holder on the seat, brought her back to her senses.

"Really?" she asked.

"What do you think? I am joking? I don't fool around about my living. It's the thing that brings food on my plate and joy to my soul. I can never imagine lying about it," he patted his cheeks like asking for forgiveness from god. "And by the way, just because I lied to you once, it doesn't mean I always lie and that I'm a bad guy, okay. If you don't believe me, you can take a look at my bag." he patted the rolls of paper that were peeping out as proof.

Automatically her eyes snapped at his bag. "What do you draw?" she then asked.

"Well, I draw landscapes, misty mornings, birds, animals or anything to do with nature. But my specialization is portraits."

"Why portraits, any special reason?"

"Well, I think portraits have that unique ability to express the person's manners or their inner feelings or expressions on paper. They are very challenging to draw as well, though I have done hundreds of them. Besides, I draw whatever pleases my eyes. If I like the look and shape. I simply draw, don't ponder much." He shrugged. For the first time, she looked at him with a genuine interest and after a moment, she asked, "What about me? Do you like how I look? I mean, would you like to draw me if given the chance?" she asked.

Avinash was taken aback. The whole world around him went mute. Although the bus was filled with noisy passengers' chatter, the conductor's impatient yells, only the girls voice began ringing in his ears, if only he wasn't mistaken about what she had just said. Did she just ask him if he'd like to draw her in her light, sweet voice? Well, no wonder, he had always been fascinated with her lovely long hair from the moment he met her. But now, sitting next to her, up close, he stole a long glance at her. Her face was a perfect round, just like the full moon, skin as smooth and flawless like it was dipped in a silky liquid. And those eyes were like someone had glued two large, round chocolates under the perfectly arched brows.

"I'd love to," he said in a very low voice, followed by silence.

Minutes later, Avinash and the girl got down at the next stop where there was a nearby park to make her wish come true. He didn't bother if he'd reach late to college; his mind was filled with a strong desire to make a beautiful portrait.

The girl sat on a low rock, one leg bent on the other knee, under the shade of a huge coral wood tree, hands clutched around the knees. Her long hair was open, flowing down, its curly ends dancing on her thighs, just as Avinash had suggested. Her dupatta that was wrapped around her neck fluttered gently with the flowing breeze. Her big chocolate-like eyes were wide open, rarely blinking, her posture still as though posing for a perfect pose. She looked like a historical princess, clad in modern clothes, which reminded him of an illustration in a glossy book. Avinash sat down on the grass, armed with all the necessary tools to depict the beauty in front of him. For the next hour, his neck was bent over a sheet of paper clamped on a pad resting on his thigh, his fingers moving gracefully across the paper. He was flicking his eyes between the girl and the pad, engrossed in depicting the delicacy of her. The park had been filled with the noisy chatter of children, couples and families who were out for their day of fun. But nothing seemed to ruin his concentration, not even the prickling sensation under his bum, for he'd been doing this for years and years. Above all, the girl's strange charm wasn't letting him put down the pencil, pulling him like a solid magnet.

After raking his eyes between the paper and the girl, his brow furrowed in immense rapture, there it was. The white sheet was covered with the beautiful drawing of the girl. When he looked at it, he had a feeling that out of all the drawings he'd done by far, this was the best. "Here you go," he said and handed the rolled sheet to the girl, who was curiously waiting,

She quickly unrolled the sheet. She then gave a gasp of awe. She was overwhelmed and speechless. The drawing he made looked more beautiful than she actually was. How could he do that? She thought admiringly.

Avinash was eagerly waiting for her response, his hands clamped over his back, tapping impatiently. 'Awesome,' 'splendid,' 'masterful' – all these terms were tossing inside his head that were about to flow from the girl's mouth anytime. Come on, quick, say something, he screamed silently, looking at her. But strangely, she stuffed the drawing into her bag without a single word, like she had been suppressing her delight. Why did she do that? Maybe she needed a little nudge or a kick-start and then he could hear all those possible compliments he was waiting for.

"So?" he said, suggestively. "What do you think?"

The girl completely ignored him, like she hadn't even heard him.

"Thanks a lot," she said, not even looking at him, busily gathering all her belongings as though the business had ended and she had to leave.

Ouch, that stung him. And wasn't that rude? Just 'Thanks a lot?' Simple thanks couldn't end their acquaintance. He needed more. More words, more compliments and, above all, a little step forward in their new friendship. Someone in her place would have jumped up and down in excitement like a kid gifted with bags full of chocolates, or may be hug him. Okay, at least jump for sure. All those beautiful terms he fantasized were fast flying out of his head like bees in different directions.

"I've to dash, I'm afraid," the girl said, checking if she had shoved all her things back in to her back.

Something inside Avinash's heart flipped. 'To where, a high class cocktail meeting or a ramp walk?' he wanted to snap, though he stifled the words before they came out.

She then suddenly snapped her head up at him as though she read his thoughts and was about to say something. A hope surged in his heart. But the next moment, she held her head low, "Did I miss anything?" she was talking to herself.

Damn, Avinash had a sudden vision of screaming at the top of his lungs, snatching the drawing from her hands and ripping it to pieces. Though in reality, he plastered a fake smile.

Millions of questions ran in his head. Didn't she like the drawing? Or had she no sense of gratitude, or was she really that busy? But come on, no matter what, she should at least thank the person who fulfilled her sudden dream. Was what he to her? A street artist? Thank god, she didn't fling a coin at him as a reward.

"You're welcome," he literally forced the words out of his mouth with hurt pride. At least if she didn't have the gratitude to say thanks, he'd say 'welcome' to feed his own hurt pride.

And the girl walked away, almost running without a backward glance, as though the stock market would collapse if she didn't rush. Avinash stood there, his face fallen, watching her go, just the way he did on the night he had first met her. So much for thinking he was a genius in dealing with girls. Their acquaintance still remained the same, strangers, he thought with a pang!

That night, when the entire city fell asleep, the clouds floating past the full moon in the sky, stars twinkling bright, Avinash wriggled in his bed like never before. Normally, he would fall asleep as soon as his head hit the pillow, but today, he couldn't! Sleep felt like a faraway dream. The girl stole it. He was furious at her for having left him in the park and walking off without showing any gratitude. He was clueless why he couldn't get over the fact that she had already left from his life even before any acquaintance and that he had no option except to accept it. But he simply couldn't let her go off his mind. He swore he'd never speak to her if he chanced upon her again. But, would he really cross her path? He didn't even know her name. The secret truth was that he desperately wanted to see her again, talk to her and hear a few compliments to feed his ego, though he knew no such thing would happen. Then a brilliant thought crept into his mind. He knew it was a stupid thing to even think about it, but he couldn't help it. Before he stopped himself, he slipped from the bed silently and headed towards his bag under the dimly-lit hall. He then pulled out a paper, pad and a few pencils, tucked them under his arm and went straight into the kitchen. Dropping down to the cool floor tiles, he took a deep breath and bent his head over the sheet, his inner voice guiding as he moved the pencil. His back arched for the next few hours, brow knitted as he worked on the crisp, white sheet. Occasionally, he'd close his eyes tight, tapping his chin with the pencil, his mind working hard and hard reminiscing about her features. It was tough and weary drawing someone from just a memory. Whenever he felt the portrait unturned to his expectations, he'd strike the entire drawing without a tinge of guilt and then start again on a fresh paper. After spending scrupulous hours, his hands freely moving against the paper, his bruised ego slowly waned away, and was replaced with a joyful pride. Finally he was able to give a face, a face of the girl.

Sahas sleepily watched his friend from his bed but didn't bother to call at him or ask him what he was doing. He had gotten used to his friend's strange behaviour of waking up in the middle of the night and drawing something. His friend must have been suffering from a blind drawing disease, just like blind walking.

Once he was done, Avinash ran his slim fingers over the girl's picture. Wow, he made it. It looked so real and vivid as though it wasn't a drawing but the tiny, replica image of the girl, resting in his palms, staring back at him. It was simply perfect. By far, there was only one person whom he could draw from imagination, his friend Sahas. But now, with this achievement, the number had risen to two.

Avinash bent over the girl's drawing and inhaled the scent of ink deeply. His nostrils stood erect as though he had smelled thousands of exotic flowers at once.

"Who are you?" he whispered, staring at her as though she had come to him for real. His heart was at once filled with irresistible pleasure.

Mount Victoria College had been jazzed up like a new bride. All the blocks were festooned with beautifully coloured banners and the classrooms looked perfectly clean like never before. The college's Annual Day celebrations were to be held the following day and students had been busy rehearsing for their respective events. Excitement and joyful activities were visible all around.

Sahas sat on the edge of big stage that had been draped with shades of beige and white curtains, bright lights hanging from the corners. He clamped a long paper in his hands and had been reciting the welcome speech that he was to deliver the next day. Given the fact he wasn't a public speaking pro, he had still stepped forward, and much to his joy, had been selected out of ten freshers to give the speech. Actually, living with his friend in Bangalore from the past two weeks had brought remarkable change in him. He became more open, a little candid in his nature and had been utterly relishing the new college and the city. He was thrilled to bits by this new opportunity which would be challenging, and who knew, even a life-changing event. He could shed off his shyness and stage fear, could make more friends or could possibly grab many more opportunities in the near events. Though he was all nervy and tensed all along, he had been practising the speech several times.

After practice, he met the cultural coordinator, Professor Mohul, for the final nod of approval. Also, he had said that he'd give him the guests' names with their professions for him to address at the beginning of the speech.

Sahas rapped at the professor's half-open door, poked his head around and asked if he could get inside.

Professor Mohul had perched on a black leather chair, his head bent over some documents spread across his table. He snapped his head up. "Ah, Sahas, come inside. Is the speech ready?" He had said that he believed Sahas had an unspoken goal and grit determination in life and hence had given him a chance to prove himself.

Sahas walked towards his table. "Yes sir, I am done. I want you to have a look at it for the final approval," he handed the paper to him and crossed his hands over his chest. Professor adjusted his glasses on the bridge of his nose before skimming through it. He suggested a couple of final changes and said that he counted on him and that Sahas should perform well. Later, he pulled the drawer, took a paper out from it and handed it to Sahas. "Here is the list of guests to be addressed before the speech. Try not to make any mistakes, okay."

Sahas nodded and reached out for the paper as the Professor went on asking about other issues if he had been facing any. He had been so friendly and supportive all through the process, unlike others. Sahas felt a swell of respect for him and swore to meet his expectations. He couldn't stop marveling at the fortune he'd been given. Asking for anything more would only be petty.

"Well, take a look at the guest list and let me know if you have any queries." Professor said.

Sahas enthusiastically peered at the guests who had been invited for the next day's programme, his fingers snail crawling on the paper. Suddenly, his face turned chalk white, finger paused at one particular guest name. Sahas narrowed his eyes and read again making sure he wasn't mistaken. No, he wasn't. He sure remembered his name, the name that could bring to life all his nightmares buried deep within. His hands quivered and so did the list in his hand. His knees felt so weak, he couldn't stand anymore.

"Are you okay?" professor asked startled.

"I …I… I don't know sir." Sahas's voice shook.

"Please sit down for a minute and rest," the Professor said, pouring him a glass of water from the bottle on his table. "Here you go!"

Sahas dropped down on the seat quickly. The guest list in his hands was still trembling. When he reached for the glass with another hand, he winced as though he was lifting a bucket load of water. He gulped down the water and took a few breaths to calm down.

"What happened suddenly? Didn't you have your breakfast?" Professor was looking at him worryingly.

Sahas shook his head, peered at the guest list once again and took a moment before asking him, flinched. "Sir, is Dayanand one of the guests tomorrow?" Even uttering his name felt disgraceful.

The professor leaned forward, his elbows resting on the table. "You mean Dayanand, CEO of Rota India?"

Sahas nodded his head silently, making thousand silent prayers to god under his breath. 'Please have him say no.'

"Yes, of course," professor shrugged apparently. "He's a high profile business tycoon in our city. Besides, he funds our college every year. But why?"

Sahas's heartbeat almost stopped. His fingers which he had crossed under the table tightened with fury. No matter how much he tried to stifle the emotions, they crawled up on his face and sat tight: Wrath, hate, fright. Professor looked at him puzzled, watching the weirdly changing emotions on his student's face. "What's wrong?"

Sahas shook his head helplessly. No matter how hard he tried to strangle the words in his mouth, they spat out. "Then, I'm sorry sir. I don't think I can give the speech."

"But why?" Professor was taken aback.

Sahas felt a swell of sorry and sympathy towards his sir. He had been trying to help and encourage the village boy, but what had he done? "I just can't, I am really sorry. I can't face that man."

Here he goes! His deepest secret was almost surfacing in front of his sir.

"Any particular reason,"

A taut silence followed, but nothing came out of Sahas's mouth. He lowered his head staring at his own hands, not able to meet his sir's gaze.

The professor looked at him thoughtfully for a moment and then flapped his hand in irritation. "Ah, I got it. What I don't understand was why guys like you always find faults in other people's growth, especially great people like Dayanand. And it's not just you! He's gathered a lot of enemies in his own city," he grunted, looking into Sahas's eye challengingly. "Never mind, but if you hadn't been recommended by the same Dayanand, you would have ended up in some stupid, dilapidated government college with your background," he said 'government college' with such a distaste.

The guest list slipped down from Sahas's hand, rolled across the room and ended up at the door. But he didn't bother to glance or pick it up. His world had suddenly turned upside down. It wasn't just a shock, but a whipped blow as though someone had whacked his face with a ton of bricks. Or rather that would have been much better. So the college seat he had dreamt of wasn't the result of his hard work, but had been thrown at him by someone's mercy, that too from the person he had hated all his life. So much for thinking the professor was being supportive. All his dreams and hopes had been shattered to pieces. Damn the speech, damn the college and damn Bangalore. He couldn't stay in the room for a minute more; in fact, not even in the college. It was like standing on fireballs. He rose from his chair abruptly, wrenching thoughts running in his head and soon walked away, not bothering even for a proper excuse.

Rota India was one of Bangalore's renowned software companies. Within a short time, it had developed into a large organization and began extending its branches across other cities as well. Soon, it went on to become a roaring success with the given stiff competition. Although its reputation had been built on the hard work of hundreds of its employees, no one denied that a major reason for its success was the company's employer, the managing director and CEO, Dayanand. When he had been passed down the company assets by his father that was full of debts, almost in a closing down condition, things had been tough. He re-started from scratch, with very a few employees and nothing expect unflinching determination. Fellow businessmen and critics expressed that the company couldn't withstand the stiff competition and a sound businessman would probably shut it down. But Dayanand never feared, or paid heed to their opinions. He went on to storm the weathers and raised the company bit by bit, shutting down all the mouths who spoke behind his back.

It was a warm afternoon, the sun still in the sky. Atmosphere inside the Rota India was familiarly busy, employees charged up with energy. The office was filled with the shrill taps on computers. Inside the meeting room, it was much more energetic than outside. Few employees, who sat around the oval table, untouched glasses of water in front of them, were staring at the screen filled with long zigzag lines indicating some data. Standing on the podium, beside an upholstered task chair, was a tall, sturdy man in an expensive suit. His posture was upright, voice vibrant and shrill. Nobody who'd never known him could have guessed he was in his early fifties.

"So, in this stiff market where threats block all yours paths, how do we go forward…" he was saying as all the employees in the room listened to his every word with rapt attention. Some among them were dreaming to be like him one day.

He was Mr Dayanand – brilliant, unpredictable and hardworking, the one who often made headlines in the local newspapers as a big shot. But only few people knew that he was both respected and hated equally for his dedication and the stern business decisions he usually took.

Sahas didn't know what poked him to go to the office that day: Anger, frustration, fear or rage that had been bottling up for years, or worse, all? But from the time he had arrived in Bangalore, he hoped that he would never encounter this person in his life. But unfortunately, destiny had put a lazy finger in his life and twirled it sharply that he couldn't help but meet this person. When he reached Rota India, his face was boiling hot. He enquired about Dayanand at the reception, his fingers drumming impatiently on the table. The elegantly dressed lady who sat behind the reception politely informed him that the person he was looking for was in an important meeting and that he needed a prior appointment to meet him. With the limited patience he had, Sahas forcefully nodded and asked her for directions to the meeting room. Before she ushered him to the sitting area, he headed towards the room with huge strides at lightning speed, ignoring the yells of the receptionist from behind. Marching past the gob-smacked faces of the staff, he almost took to running and reached the meeting room without being caught. He didn't bother to follow the etiquettes of rapping on the door, simply pushed it open with a swish. The cool air from inside the room splashed on his face as he stood still.

All heads in the room snapped around, looking at the guy in his filthy clothes, the one who seemed to have dropped from another planet, except for Dayanand. Though his face registered surprise, an invisible delight that no one could recognize flashed. There was a still silence. Sahas felt paralyzed with fear. What was he doing? He suddenly thought, outrage slowly dying away.

Where did he think he had come to? He wasn't about to do the talking to some random person. We're talking about Dayananad, one of the most powerful, strong and influential people in the city.

Or, a cruel, vicious person, Sahas thought gravely. If he stepped back cowardly, then he wouldn't forgive himself ever.

Just then, a guard dashed in from behind. He caught Sahas's collar and pulled him as he jerked away from the room, ready to be kicked out like a rag bag, or worse, end up in jail. But no! Nothing like that happened. The guard slowly loosened his grip around Sahas's collar. All eyes averted from him to Dayanand, who stretched his finger at the guard, flipping no, his eyes unreadable. The room had fallen ghostly silent.

Sahas wriggled his shirt and took steps towards Dayanand. He no more looked like a timid college boy with years of cocooning in his mother's embrace. He looked fierce, eyes red with rage. All the words he had been practicing for years, the moment he'd been awaiting, was a few steps away.

"Who the hell do you think you are?" Sahas finally said, finding his voice. "How dare you to get me admission into the college? What do you think you were doing, bestowing your humanity on me? Just go to hell!" His balled fists cradled on his thighs trembled slightly. But he didn't stop.

A dense silence followed. Dayanand closed his eyes as if he had heard something terrible. His face was unreadable, yet flooding with plethora of emotions. Pain, agony, or guilt, nobody knew, except him.

Not able to defy the insult hurled at his employer, one of them stood up ready to throw this cod out of the room. He looked at his boss for a flicker of an approval. But Dayanand stood silently still, his eyes staring into the distance at nothing, as if he had turned deaf.

Sahas went on, "The admission you got me is like a rag doll torn into bits by street dogs. Now don't you ever dare to interfere in my life again," he thundered, his voice echoing across the room. And then he walked off. That's it.

Everything happened in a jiffy. The room turned to hushing voices, people astonished at what had just happened. But nobody dared to speak. Dayanand still stood rooted in his place like a wax statue. He wasn't furious. There was only one emotion written on his face – guilt. But no one could read it, because he was known as a man with zero emotions.

Finally, one employee dared to stand. "Sir, who the hell is that bastard and why were you silent? Just give me permission, I'll go and smash his head," he couldn't hold back anger. Normally he would never have raised his voice before his boss, but the dishonour had made him forget office etiquette.

Dayanand at last dragged his eyes unwillingly and looked at his employee. A tinge of embarrassment, something the staff saw rarely, flashed. Everyone was curious to hear him.

"He's my son!" he said in a voice that only he could hear.

Sahas didn't know what exactly he was feeling at the moment as he was heading back to his room. His body shook uncontrollably and he felt terrible. Although he had spurted dialogues that worked well in the movies, he cursed himself for having confronted Dayanand. Even his shadow felt toxic to him. He had never wanted to meet him or hear his name. In fact, this was the first time he had come face to face with him. He'd only seen Dayanand in the photos shown to him by Baba, an old well-wisher of their family. This was the reason why Sahas never wanted to come to Bangalore. Earlier, he had felt that he could root this man out of his life, just the way he had done, but now after this encounter, he felt helpless, years of buried memories resurfacing. Tears welled up in his eyes. It was like he had unlocked the room of memories for which he'd lost the key many years before. He collapsed on the bed, his face down. He then cried and cried, years of suppressing emotions turning into unstoppable tears. Dayanand was always just a cruel man to him; he could never think of him as his father, even in his wildest dreams. To him, he was a dead man and that was what her mother had told him as a child.

It was Baba, who helped Sahas and his mother at their hotel. He took care of them as if they were his own family. He was the one who had told him about Dayanand. He'd narrated how curious, enthusiastic, young Dayanand was with loads of energy when he'd visited their village, Augumbe for some project work. He then fell in love with Sahas's mom and would deliberately come to the hotel to catch a glimpse of the young woman. Even Sahas's mom had felt the same for him. Things went well until she became pregnant. And then, all hell broke loose when he left her in lurch and ran away like a coward. Sahas had listened to the entire story with clenched fists, wishing he could knock down the teeth of Dayanand right away. But nonetheless, he never discussed anything with his mother as he couldn't see her hurt. That story had been imprinted on his conscious mind and he vowed never to confront or forgive Dayananand in his life.

But why did he want to come back into their lives now, all of a sudden? How dare he get him the admission into college? What did all of this mean now, after scores of years? Was he trying to make up for all those lost years? Many unanswered questions rattled Sahas's mind.

It was a beautiful evening. The sun went down the horizon, enveloping the city in a golden glow. The ground opposite Avinash's room was filled with many people, mainly youngsters, who were playing football. Sahas sat on a low step at the corner of the playground, away from people's sight. It had almost been a week since he encountered Dayanand and still he wasn't able to come out of the shock. He stopped going to college too. Sahas had been spending most the days either sleeping in the room or sitting in the ground doing nothing. He felt utterly lonely inside the house after his friend had left for work. He thought watching people would lift the sorrow, but no, nothing seemed to fill the void inside his heart, which with every passing day was growing like a large black hole.

A ball came rolling towards Sahas. The boys shouted at him to throw back the ball to them, but Sahas didn't seem to hear them. He was lost in his own thoughts, eyes distant and weary. And then, a rugged figure who had been watching Sahas from so long lifted the ball and threw it back to the boys. It was Avinash who having walked into the empty room had guessed without much difficulty that his friend would be sitting outside, doing nothing.

He sank down next to Sahas and watched his hollow eyes and sunken temples in a moment of silence. For the last ten days, he'd been witnessing his friend's self-torment. Sahas had stopped talking to everyone, including him. He hadn't even had a decent meal for a week. Every morning he'd get up with sore eyes that screamed he had cried all night. Avinash had tried like hell to cheer his friend up, and to know what exactly it was that was bothering him. But Sahas never uttered a word about it. He had always bottled up all his emotions until they suddenly burst out like a volcano one day. But today, he wouldn't give up, Avinash swore. "Will you please tell me what is bothering you," he tried again.

Sahas shook his head. "Nothing, just not feeling well."

Avinash couldn't hold back the smirk at the usual response he had been hearing for last couple of days. "Oh please Sahas, don't give the same, repeated story. I'm fed up of hearing about it. Do you even realize there was a ball lying next to you and those guys have been shouting at you? And you sat here like a rock, sorry, a deaf rock, saying you're not well," he snapped with mild irritation. "Look at you man. How many times had I told you not to bottle up your emotions and that isn't good for you? But you never listen to me. Sometimes you make me wonder if I am your friend or just a roommate you have nothing to say to, except obvious hellos."

Sahas looked down at his foot, scraping the sand.

Avinash wondered if even he had listened to him or not. "Look, if you have been homesick or something, take a break, visit mom and stay there for a while. Else, kindly open up and share your anguish. I might not help the way you imagine, but it'd definitely lessen your anguish."

Still silence.

"Okay, I thought I could convince you and help you out. But you see, I can't do it without your support. Now please stop this silent treatment and say something. You're wracking my brain." he begged, his eyes pleading. "Else I'd call mum and tell what you're up to." The words shot out of his mouth.

Sahas snapped his eyes from the ground and locked them with his friend. He could do nothing except marvel at the way his friend had been struggling to cheer him up for days. But the fact was, he was too terrified to share this one, big secret. He was afraid that people would take his grief lightly and brush it aside. Not that his friend would do the same. But how long would Sahas carry the burden of this secret. Sooner or later, he had to disburden the torment he'd been going through.

He took a deep breath, locked his eyes at the faraway tree and took a moment before blurting out. "I saw someone whom I swore never to meet." He finally broke the silence.

"And who's that?"

"The one who was responsible for bringing me to earth, the one whom I've hated all my life, the one who'd left me and my mom before I was born and the one who'd run away from us like a coward,"

For the next hour, Sahas recited the whole story, the one that had been churning inside his heart, giving him sleepless nights.

Avinash listened with rapt attention, his fingers crossed. Every once and then he glanced up at Sahas, shocked and pained, at the new revelations. Sahas had never spoken about his dad to anyone, and if someone would ask him questions about him, he'd stop talking to them forever. Although Avinash had smelled that something was wrong from his childhood days, he never pussy-footed into his friend's personal life. He accepted him for what he was and was glad he did it. Now, this sudden, astonishing news made him shift uncomfortably in his place. He couldn't imagine Sahas's plight and felt sorry for him. Though his own parents fought every now and then, they'd patch up at the end of the day. But this seemed horrendous. He sympathized with Sahas and wished he hadn't pressed him much for stirring up painful memories. Also, he felt a swell of anger at Dayanand, whom he pictured as a vicious villain. He swore to knock his teeth down when he met him. His friend had every right to be both angry and sad.

But was not going to college and punishing himself the right solution for the problem? Avinash thought hard.

After Sahas finished, a taut silence followed. Avinash didn't know what to say. He first stood up, took a few steps around the ground, pondering and then sat back down, turning to his friend.

"Sahas, I cannot pretend to know the pain you're going through, because only the person who is in such a situation can feel the real pain. But do ask yourself a few questions. You never wanted to end up in Bangalore, but here you are. You never wanted to see that hated man in your life, but you have. So, nothing can stop you from walking on the path that fate has decided for you. And you can't change things by punishing yourself. I bet you would have nailed the admission without any individual's intervention. You're capable of that. Not just now, but right from your childhood days. You're hardworking, determined and have great zeal to do something." He slowly threw his arm around Sahas. "Look, you've already seen enough pain in your life, now you deserve a good education. Please continue your college and make people proud of your success. In the midst of all this, have you ever thought about mom? Don't you know how hard it was for her to send her only son faraway to the city in the hope that one day he'd make her proud?"

Sahas looked pained. He had never thought about it. Yes, if he'd gone to his village, sure his mother would have been happy, but only from outside. Deep within, she'd have been torn to bits. He had a sudden flash of her crouching at the cooking pot, blowing in to the pipe, thick smoke gushing up, her lungs filled with dust. Tears swelled in his eyes. She had been working day and night just for him, to give him good education. He felt a flicker of guilt and lowered his head.

Avinash looked at him as though he could read his mind. "Now you have two options. 1) Blank out that bloody Dayanad from you memory, or 2) Down the street, a new book stall has opened, where I'm sure you'd get one on 'how to put a hex on powerful business magnets to drown them into debts.' We'll buy that. I'll accompany you so that we both read and practice, what say?" he stared at Sahas wide-eyed.

Despite the urge to cry, Sahas laughed out loud. "I prefer the second option."

"That sounds like my real friend."

A week later, one lazy afternoon, while all the staff members in the college had had their lunch and gone back to their work, Avinash stood on a ladder in the library, tidying up the upper zone of the history block. He had intended to do it from a week, but felt so lazy. Now that all the books were disorganized and was taking ages for him to pull the required one, he launched in to cleaning. Just as he was about to finish, he was interrupted by his co-librarian. "Someone is asking for you," the guy shouted.

Avinash supposed it was Sahas whom he had asked to come to the library whenever he was feeling a little low by making a prior call. But not a problem, Avinash knew that though his friend was flaunting an air of jaunty confidence, pretending to be fine, he was broken to bits inside.

As he got down the ladder, Avinash mentally hatched a quick plan on how to cheer his friend up. Perhaps, he'd take permission for an hour or so and take him somewhere. He walked to the main area of the library with a few books clutched in his hands. Placing them on the desk, he glanced around for his friend, but when his co-librarian's finger lazily stretched out at a corner table, he was surprised, his posture little swayed. It took him a moment to register.

It wasn't Sahas. It was the long-haired girl looking in the line of his direction over the magazine she was leafing through. She placed it on the desk and stood up to greet him.

"Hi, how have you been?"

Avinash was taken aback. He'd never anticipated such a surprise visit. Not that he didn't like it, his heart had already starting doing bungee jumps inside. But it was beyond his senses how the girl whom he thought would never ever meet him had turned up in his library out of the blue? Had she come here for some work and had bumped into him? He opened his mouth, but words were planets distant.

"You're here…" he said, but the rest of the phrase hung in the air when the girl chirped in saying,

"I'm here to meet you."

"To meet me?"

"Yes, absolutely, you heard me right. Just to meet you."

Avinash wished that the whole library would close its eyes for a moment so that he could do a little jig to convey how happy he was. But he kept his smile firm, for a tinge of ego rose from nowhere.

"So, what brought you here?" he said nonchalantly, like he wasn't surprised or delighted at her visit.

The girl shifted on her foot. "I heard your canteen serves good coffee. Can we talk there?" she smiled.

They both sat opposite to each other, having the piping hot coffee, still silence between them. "So, how have you been?" she asked.

"Good," Avinash gave a curt reply, took a sip of coffee. "How did you find me?" he asked slowly, though this wasn't the way he wanted it to go. He stifled the urge to flood her with his mind wracking questions standing on the table and yelling. 'How did you find me? How did you know where I have been working? What made you come here?' But he didn't want to sound desperate for he might frighten her and she might run away like earlier, or worse, never come back again. He needed to play it cool.

"It wasn't that difficult," she shrugged, taking a sip of her coffee, "That night when you helped me with the goons, if you recall, I was standing at the bus stand near this college. Since there were no other offices or colleges located in this area, it's obvious you work somewhere around." She made it sound very intelligent. And then after a moment, she added, "By the way, your drawing sheet had a stamp of your college on it." She grinned. "When I came here, I asked for the guy who makes portraits, the women especially. They said I can find you in the library."

All the rainbow colours were painted on Avinash's face. "Very cool," nobody could empathize the word 'cool' like him. So, the girl had not just used her brain, but had struggled to come all this way to meet him. He was impressed. But why had she took the struggle now and ignored him then? He asked her the same.

"I was in a little hurry that day and I didn't want to thank you for the drawing in a rushed manner."

"So?" He swallowed, his ears highly alert.

The girl took another sip, put down the tumbler and sat back on the chair, her eyes beaming. "What can I say?" she cleared her throat, "You're awesome. You have an amazing and incredible talent. And that drawing of mine is hypnotic and marvellous. I look at it all the time. I can't tell you how many times I have seen it. I have shown it to my friends as well and no doubt they fell in love with it too. Now, they also want to be drawn by you," she smiled, moving her hands furiously up and down to convey her state of fascination. "And you know, every time I look at it, it makes me realize how beautiful I am...." she was unstoppable.

Avinash's heart was filled with heavenly pride. Nobody had praised his skill in such lovely words. People simply picked up his drawings and said 'thanks' or 'lovely' and walked away, just the way she had done once. No wonder he'd desperately wanted to hear from her. Look at her compliments, the way her eyes were twinkling, hands making circles, words blowing out like rustling wind, lips forming impossible twists. Her lips, wow, they looked as fresh as morning dew. He couldn't decide whether she looked more beautiful in the picture or in real life. The afternoon sunlight that was slanting through the window they sat nearby made her skin look luminous and golden. What is happening to me? Avinash wondered. "I think you need to pause now. My praise barometer can't take too much reading. I fear it will make my chest explode and my shirt would be torn in pride," he chuckled and they both broke into laughter.

"You are funny."

"No seriously, thank you for all those compliments. No one has praised me like you have. I'm impressed, no…" he shook his head. "I'm flattered." he blushed, revealing his white teeth.

"You're welcome. You're worth more than that, in fact. But I'm a little curious to know how you do it with such perfection." Avinash's tone suddenly took on the seriousness of a professional artist, something that seldom happened when someone asked him about his talent. He rested his elbows on the table and leaned forward. "All I do is observe the minutest of details of what I see," he said, watching her thick lashes, the innocent eyes kohled in dark eyeliner, and the small dot sitting between her brows. He wondered absently why the world around him went invisible in her presence. What was this mysterious, magnetic pull she had? The drawing he had done of her the night when he couldn't sleep sprang up in his mind. For a moment he debated if he should tell her about it. No, definitely not now, he shrugged off the thought. What would she think of him? A crazy maniac who's fond of girls? He didn't want to nip the relationship in the bud just as it was beginning to bloom.

"I've heard that artists have beautiful, thick lines on their palms. Do they?" she asked him curiously.

Avinash smiled. "You speak like an astrologer. Some people even mythify that only left handed people can become artists. But seriously, I am not aware of all those things. The only thing I ever learned in my life with perfection is drawing. I just love to draw and that I do. That's it."

The girl nodded. "My friend is in to arts too. She writes poems," she said sweetly.

"Oh really?"

"Do you like to read poems?" she asked curiously.

"Of course, I do. Who doesn't like them?" The girl took a long time in tucking a wisp of hair behind her ear like she was buying some time. "Great, my friend actually wrote a poem on the drawing of me, the one you drew. Would you like to see it?"

"I would love to."

Excitingly, she pulled out the rolled drawing from inside her bag and spread it on the table, facing his side. She placed a pitcher as weight on the edge of it. There were a few slanting lines written down in bold letters just below the drawing.

Like a welcome summer rain, like a bright sun on a rainy day, like a star filled sky, she sat on a rock amid bushes. And on that rosy cheek, so soft and fluffy like a wisp of cotton tinted a glow...

Avinash bent his head and studied the lines carefully, like a scientist. The girl stared at him, unblinking, furiously chewing her nails. A moment later, she asked, "What do you think?"

Avinash pondered for a while, but said nothing. He then gave her an inquisitive stare. "Can I look at your hand?" he asked. The girl hesitantly stretched her hand towards him.

He took her hands into his, his eyes glued at them, assessing like a real astrologer. "I think your friend has many beautiful thick lines across her palms," he ran his fingers gently on hers, instantly feeling electric by the touch. "What do you say?" he raised his brows at her.

"I'll let you know after your comments," she looked at him in the eyes.

"If someone asked me to judge the poem, I'd select it for a first prize."

The girl dropped her head shyly and grinned. She then glanced back at him. "Thanks. You guessed it right," she blushed bewitchingly. "I am the friend who wrote that. I write poems. I love to do that, especially looking at drawings. That's the reason I didn't thank you properly that day. I wanted my poem to be a gift to you, to say how much I loved your drawing, and in return, I was expecting another beautiful picture of mine from you."

Avinash was still holding her hand. His instinct was to squeeze it fondly, but he simply patted her on the wrist and let it go with a smile. "Of course, it'd be my privilege to draw you again." How could he even think she had no gratitude. How stupid of him! What a lovely girl and a lovely gift. He felt instantly connected to her like they'd known each other from ages. Was it her charm or the way she spoke or the mysterious aura surrounding her, he wasn't sure. But he liked her very much.

"You sure it didn't sound like the one blowing their own trumpet, the poem, I meant?" she grinned.

Avinash shook his head. "Absolutely not."

Soon, they were chatting away, uninhibitedly discussing their interests, enjoying each other's company. Sometimes, with like-minded people and beautiful souls, time cannot be measured. Avinash had a feeling that if the world was a tick tock clock, he'd pause it and simply stare at her.

"So, what's your name?" he finally asked her, taking a sip of his third cup of coffee… or fourth?

It had been nearly two weeks Sahas went back to college. Now, walking on the familiar campus past a couple of known faces, he felt a little embarrassed. Despite his friend's long lecture on the importance of education to boost his confidence, he couldn't overcome the fears. Sitting in the class felt like sitting on thorns. He suddenly became self conscious of his presence in the class, as though fellow students were muttering behind his back, gossiping about his sudden disappearance. Or worse, the fear that someone would pry him with uncomfortable questions about his admission through a big shot.

But all his unfounded fears and imaginations were put to end when no such thing happened. People were pretty busy with their own problems and no one had even noticed his absence for a long time. The truth was that he had never asserted his presence in the class and had always isolated himself by sitting in a corner. After two classes, during the break, he rushed outside, heading straight to the sprawling lawn. He didn't bother to go the canteen either as it teemed with students. All he wanted was a little space and a little peace which he knew he could get only at the lawn.

He sat on an empty bench shaded under a huge neem tree and glanced around. Much to his pleasure, there were no people around, except for the few studious students who were seriously engrossed in their books and wouldn't lift their heads unless some disaster like an earthquake shook them. Feeling a little cheerful, he flipped open the Accounts book that he hadn't touched for many days. Minutes later, when he was totally submerged, a soft, familiar voice broke his attention from the book. He snapped his head up.

It was Aarti, his only friend in the college who stopped by to say hi on spotting him on the way to her class. She was standing tall, a few books clutched in her arms, her face filled with joy on seeing him.

"Hi," he greeted her.

"Long time, no see huh. So nice to see you," she said, casually dropping down beside him on the bench.

Sahas wriggled in his seat, a little nervous. He felt too scared and anxious around girls. Back in his village, even in their small hotel, he rarely made any attempts to speak to the posh female visitors. He'd simply keep himself busy in the kitchen, cooking, while his mother did the serving. She always used to tease him about what he would do when he got married and that his wife would dominate him like hell.

"Where have you been for so many days? I've been searching for you all over the college campus. I even asked your classmates, but nobody knew where you were," Aarti asked worryingly, leaving out the fact that most of his classmates didn't even know that there was a person called Sahas in their class. "You've no idea how eagerly I waited for your speech on the Annual Day," she said, a little disappointed. "You practiced it so well. At first I thought I'd missed it, but I never saw you even later." Panic seized Sahas. He couldn't think of what to say. He swallowed hard, taking plentiful time, his mind running with best possible reasons.

"Oh, is that so? Mmm... I..." he stuttered, "I actually fell ill, so went to my village," he said, biting his tongue at his choice of words. Why would I go to my village if I fell ill!

"Oh?" She blinked, a little unconvinced, "Not a problem. I'll update you about all the cultural events and the activities that had been held. You remember about the idea of college magazine by your Accounts student? The guy received a price for his innovative idea. Not just that, there's a column called 'free speech zone' that is to get included in the magazine where one can voice their opinion on topics ranging from ragging or abuse in any form, to sanitization of bathrooms or any other issue one faced without being threatened to participate in the market of ideas. Isn't that wonderful? And then there is this...." she went on doing all the talking.

Sahas blinked uncertainly. He looked like a nervous deer that had nothing to say except nod his head. Perhaps he felt little less insecure about being a village boy. Or was it him being too hard on himself.

"By the way, you didn't ask me why I've been searching for you rigorously." She paused

"Why?" he looked at her, "You need something?"

"Well I need something for sure. It's kind of help. "She tucked some hair behind the ear. "My classmate has formed a small team of volunteers who want to spend a couple of hours a week doing social work, basically teaching underprivileged children. You see, there are many children who deserve better education, but won't get it. We're short of teachers, so I was wondering if you would like your help." She snapped her eyes at him, dripping with hope, and then shrugged, "Of course, if you are interested only. There's no push. And it will take just a couple of hours a week."

Sahas looked at her thoughtfully. So, Aarti wasn't just beautiful from outside, but inside as well. Her compassion, generosity blending with the courage to move on, stumped him. Above all, he liked the fact that she had approached him for help instead of her other friends.

"That is a very noble job you've chosen. What kind of teaching do you plan to do, by the way?" he enquired.

"A person can choose his subject of interest. Besides, we teach children up till the tenth class, so I don't think it will be difficult for our age group to teach any subject."

Sahas tapped his fingers on the book he was clutching, lost in his own thoughts."Can I suggest something?"

"Yes of course!"

"Apart from teaching, it would be nice if you guys could also instruct them on cleanliness, inculcating good habits, importance of education, etc."

"Whoa, that's a cool idea. We hadn't thought of that, thanks."

"I think along with education, a child should be aware about health, nutrition and other important subjects."

"You're right. I will discuss this with my team, but you didn't tell me if you're interested in joining us."

"You can count me in," Sahas smiled.

Aarti returned the smile with gratitude. "Thanks a lot. I didn't think you would say yes so quickly. It means a lot."

"I was born and brought up in a remote village, Aarti, and I have seen how difficult it is for children to get basic education, their basic right. It would be my pleasure to participate in something I've longed for since my childhood days."

Aarti casted a warm glance in admiration. "May I say, you're the most wonderful and beautiful soul I've ever met in our college?"

The look gave him jitters as he shifted in his seat. "Thank you." he flushed.

Since that day, they became inseparably good friends. Sahas, who usually shied away from girls, slowly started to enjoy her company. They went to the schools and worked together as a team. Though it scared him a little, being close to her, she undoubtedly made him comfortable around her. He was no more a loner without any friends. He noticed that she yearned for his company more than anyone else's. After teaching, they'd head to a nearby café and enjoy talking for hours, getting to know each other. His heart fluttered at this new, hypnotic intimacy that made him wonder if she more than liked him. But he'd done nothing except be himself to earn her attention. Perhaps, girls like it that way. Or perhaps, it was him who was putting too much meaning into the interaction with a girl who just wanted to be his friend. Whatever the reasons, he enjoyed her company and they were often spotted around the campus, leisurely strolling, bags slung across their shoulders or sitting on the rickety canteen chairs, chatting for endless hours. These had become the best moments of Sahas's life.

It was a lazy Sunday mid-morning when Avinash sauntered into his room after a lazy breakfast at the nearby hotel. The room looked lonely and boring. Although he had lived here alone for quite some years, he felt the weight of his friend's absence heavily. Sahas had gone to their village after he got a call from his mom with worrisome news that Baba had not been well. Baba had been working in their small hotel and had always been a pillar of strength for them during their ups and downs. With time, he had become a part of their family and treated Sahas like his own grandson. Besides, he didn't have a family of his own and this made the three of them much closer. Also, Sahas had been dying to see his mother since the time he had come to Bangalore. Now that his college was closed for a week for festive celebrations, he had grabbed the chance to visit his village. Avinash had wanted to accompany his friend because he too hadn't seen his family for a long time, but his college had no holidays and had to postpone the plan.

The rest of the day, Avinash set about his routines, doing them double the time he usually did on weekdays, when he'd finish the chores in frenzy. But today, he literally dragged himself for every work he did through. He played a few games with cards to kill time. When he was tired and bored, he lay on the bed; his hands clamped beneath his head and thought about some unfinished drawings he was supposed to do. But strangely, today he wasn't in the mood to work on them either. He had no other plans for a day, so thought he might steal a nap. Just as he was about to slip into slumber, the shrill voice of the mobile shook his body awake. He leapt down the bed and picked it up from the floor, assuming it to be Sahas from the village phone booth. But the next minute his face brightened as if the sun from outside had cast a glow over his face. It was a call from the long-haired girl. It was always the long-haired girl for him. In fact, he hadn't even bothered to remember her real name.

After their encounter at his college, the day after she'd surprised him with her visit, they met myriad times at his college, sometimes for a quick coffee, discussing about arts, poems, politics and many other things. Avinash found himself falling for her with every passing encounter they had. He was spell-bound, not just by her beauty, though that alone was enough to make him go crazy. But the way she countered him every time with her sound knowledge on arts, the way she tipped her head back at his silly jokes and laughed, the way her presence filled with the light, hypnotic perfume she wore, he loved everything, though he kept his feelings to himself. They had even exchanged their numbers recently. "Hi!" Avinash exclaimed over the phone, all the slumber running away.

"Hi, what are you up to? Still in the bed wriggling lazy, postponing all your works?"

He stared at his phone bewildered. Was some electronic bug implanted to it from where she could monitor all his activities? He sat straight, pulling up his pyjamas, now falling down his buttock.

"I was just guessing, okay. Now, don't you wonder and rack your brains."

Avinash heaved a sigh of relief. "So, what good my phone did to receive a call from you today?" he teased.

"Well, it's a little important, if you ask me. I want to take you somewhere important. If you're up to it, we can go," she said.

"Of course, where do you plan to take me?"

"It's a surprise. By the way, would you mind if I say I'm just a few stops away from your house," Avinash's hand tightened around the phone.

"What?" he exclaimed. Now this was the problem with her, she'd love to give surprises.

"Will that be a problem?"

"Su… sure…I meant no, of course not," he stuttered, looking around his room which was back to its messy state without his friend's ministrations. "Perfectly alright," he said, except he'd have been grateful if she had cautioned him a little earlier. "Okay, I've got to go now. Just call me if you have any trouble finding the place." he hung up quickly.

Heaving a deep sigh, he looked around. A dirty, messy, unorganized room stared back at him. From the next nano-second onwards, he wore the cap of a robot that was set to high manual speed and worked as fast as possible. He had only a few minutes and wanted his room to look splendid. Not exactly, but clean enough for a girl to step in. He couldn't bear her wrinkling her nose, saying, 'Avinash, it'd be better if we hung out at the corner café which serves nice coffee.'

Once the room was tidied up, he pulled on a pair of nicely pressed jeans and a T-shirt. He wanted to look good as well when she stepped into his house for the first time. When he was wildly raking his hair with a comb, there was a knock on the door. He froze, eyes snapped at the door. It couldn't be her. She couldn't make it this fast, no way. Well, why couldn't she? She knew every nook and cranny of Bangalore. Though he'd only once mentioned his address, he sure knew it must have got imprinted in her mind. He took a deep breath and opened the door, his heart ramming inside his chest. There she was! In all whites!

Avinash stood rooted, staring at her, wishing he could pause the moment and look at her as long as he longed.

He was never a fan of white. He always liked dark colours, deep black, deep red, deep violet. But for the first time he fell in love with white. The girl looked drop-dead gorgeous in her flowing white salwar-kameez with a matching string of pearls around her neck and beaded white bangles jingling on her wrist. A white crystal bindi dazzled like a brilliant star in the blue morning sky. Her long hair had been left open just the way he always liked. Looking at her, Avinash's fingers tingled. He stifled the urge to ask her to stand at the door for a few more minutes so that he could fetch a sheet and fill it with her drawing. What a bizarre thought!

"Will you ask me in or should I stand here the whole day like I've got a punishment," the girl teased.

Avinash grinned, shaking his thoughts away. "I'm sorry, it's just that I am too stunned to see you here," he said. "Please come in," he welcomed her.

The girl walked into his room a little embarrassed for she'd never been to his house earlier. Meeting him outside or chatting over the phone was different from being inside the closed walls with no one around. "Welcome to my paradise," he ushered her to a chair.

The girl sat and looked around. An embarrassing silence hung for a moment.

"This is a nice place you've got," she finally said.

"Thanks," he smiled, leaning against the wall, trying to look calm, though he was bubbling inside with nerves. "Last minute arrangement, else you wouldn't even dare to step in." He smiled.

"Bachelor's room huh? But it's far better than our hostel rooms."

He nodded knowingly. "So, you're here for the first time. What would you like to have?"

She thought for a moment. "Anything to drink."

"I'm afraid I never keep any alcohol at my home."

"Well, I spotted few alcohol stores on the way here," she said in a serious tone, "I wouldn't mind waiting, you know, if you plan for one," she shrugged suggestively.

"I …I think…" he stuttered when she burst out laughing, little awkwardness vanishing away between them and they were back to their friendly domain.

Later, when he stood in front of the small cupboard, his arms folded, wondering what to serve, Avinash realized how all the cooking items were neatly organized in a row. It was Sahas who had actually laboured an entire day to make the kitchen look neat and organized. In no time, the coffee tin was found. Thanks to Sahas again. He should have been here now, Avinash thought, pulling the tin off the shelf. Sahas would have darted around like a shy mouse in the small house, looking at the girl sitting in their room as though an alien from another planet had dropped by to make a documentary on them.

When Avinash opened the coffee tin, he found it nearly empty, except for a scrape of powder. He banged his head in disappointment. In his friend's absence, he hadn't been having his breakfast at home. Let alone check what was in his kitchen, since he never expected any guests to drop by. The girl had come to his house for the first time and he had to offer her something out of courtesy. He pulled the tea tin and checked inside the contents. Alas, again a scrape of powder. Half the interest he'd taken in tidying up the room and trimming himself, he should have put some in to checking what was in the kitchen, he thought, banging his head. And then suddenly something weird struck him.

When he walked back to the room with a tray of steaming cups and cookies, she was leafing through his brochure of unfinished drawings which he'd left on the bed. "Here you go," he handed her a cup.

Tending himself a cup and leaning back the wall with one of his legs bent, Avinash watched her sharply until she took a sip.

The girl furrowed her brow in confusion after taking a sip. She then stirred her drink and glanced over the rim of cup at him before taking another sip. "What's in this?" she asked him puzzled. Not that he'd put a tranquilizer in it, she trusted him more than herself.

"You like it?" he asked curiously.

"It's kind of different!" she said, the taste sinking down her throat.

Avinash gave an abashed smile. "It's cofftea," he finally said. "What?"

"It's a cofftea – combination of both coffee and tea. A special drink for a special guest."

The girl widened her eyes, not buying his words.

He shifted on his foot, embarrassed. "Well, there were only scrapings of tea and coffee left in my kitchen, so I mixed both, hoping it would be good. Sorry I didn't offer anything fancy for you. Well, it's your mistake. You should have warned me a little earlier before your visit."

"Not a problem. I'd give the menu for my next visit now. Make a note." She stretched her hands wide filling the room with twinkling of her bangles. "I'd like scallops with goat cheese with rainbow salad."

Avinash shook his head, "I don't even have a clue what you're talking about." He grinned and they burst out into laughter.

An hour later, Avinash and the girl stood in front of a massive building from where people were pouring in and out through the double gates with the catalogues clutched in their hands, hissing praises like "wonderful," "overwhelming," "splendid". Avinash's face broke open with surprise followed by a delight. He was brought to the Arts exhibition where there was going to be a display of noted artist's work from across the city.

"I read about it in today's newspaper and thought you should take a look at it." The girl smiled.

As they both made their way inside, their eyes were greeted with colourful display of varied arts ranging from pastels, water colours, pen-and-inks to photographs and pencil sketches. They walked along the aisle side by side, past art lovers who were engrossed peering at the splendid visual arts, appreciating the handiwork of contemporary artists.

Avinash nodded, fascinated. "I can see the skill and expertise in these arts. They must be noted artists."

The girl leaned in and spoke in low volume. "Every noted artist was a beginner at first. Now did you understand why I brought you here? You have a god gifted skill, Avinash. All you've do is express yourself without restraining."

Both their eyes locked and lingered for a while. The passion and energy flowing from her eyes had him spellbound. What was he to her? What good had he done to be showered with such generosity? No matter how hard he tried, he couldn't dismiss the rapt attention she was showing him.

Later, they met a couple of artists and whiled away the time chatting with them, learning their techniques and admiring the work by touring around. They even learned that the exhibition would host other activities like music and poetry writings sometimes. Avinash made a quick mental note to bring the girl and surprise her when they were to be held. It was almost evening when they left the gallery and came outside.

The weather in Bangalore was always unpredictable. It had been a sunny and hot afternoon when they walked inside the gallery, but now, out of the blue, grey clouds had sheathed the sky and it started to rain cats and dogs. They waited at the gallery hoping the rain would come to halt and then they'd make to their respective rooms. But the raindrops came down swollen and heavy. Within no time, the roads were muddy and mucky. Avinash and the girl rolled up their trousers and had to wade through knee-deep water to reach the parking lot which was only a few metres away from the gallery. Water logging had brought the evening traffic to a standstill and the roads were so congested that Avinash asked if it'd be okay for her to drop by his room as hers was farther to the other side. He promised to drop her once the rain subsided. The girl accepted with no other option. After battling two hours of brutal traffic, drenched in rain, they reached his house.

They were doused from head to toe, shaking with cold when they stepped in.

"I'll go get a towel," Avinash rushed inside, trying hard not to stare at how the wet clothes clung to her prefect curves. He soon fetched a towel and came back.

The girl had opened her long hair that swept down to her bum, tiny droplets falling from the strands onto the floor.

"Here you go," he handed her a towel and a pair of his own dry clothes. "I don't think you could stay in those wet clothes for long. You'll catch cold. So I thought these would help." He shrugged awkwardly.

The girl looked at them hesitantly.

"You can dry your own clothes and swap them when we go back to your room. I hope that's okay. Sorry to put you in trouble."

"That's okay." She smiled reaching for his dress hesitantly. If she was embarrassed, she hadn't shown it on her face.

"The bathroom is this way. I'll change and make something for us to eat. I'm ravenous. Don't expect scallops with goat cheese or something." He grinned and left her.

By the time he was back with a plate full of noodles, the only thing he was expert at, the girl emerged from the bathroom.

"Do I look like a buffoon?" she grinned awkwardly looking at the oversized t-shirt and tracks.

Avinash shook his head. "No, you look comfortable. You can run around, do impossible yoga asanas in these."

The girl smiled.

After filling their tummies with noodles, they both sat cosily beside each other, sheets of drawings spilled across their laps.

"This is one of my favourites from the recent drawings I've made," he tapped on a depiction where bunch of women clad in saris tucked behind, their backs bent from waist, worked in knee deep waters of paddy fields.

"Why?"

"It kind of reminds me of my village, the place where women work hard chopping the wood, lugging buckets of water from the well, cooking, cleaning." His eyes shone. "They are great."

"You know what I like about your drawings?" she asked, not looking up, lost in the beauty in her lap.

"What?" he whispered.

"Each one reflects a great beauty and expresses your inner self. You're a great observer, Avinash, and that seeps in each of these."

Their eyes locked and lingered for a while.

"I'm so grateful you took me to the exhibition. You're the most wonderful person I've ever met in my life." he said, taking her hands into his. The touch was electric. What was this mysterious aura spilling from her? He knew he fell in love with her the very day he met her. It took great effort to release her hands and avert his eyes from her. But strangely, the girl didn't withdraw. Instead, she tightened her grip around his and locked her eyes with him. Before he knew what he was doing, he pulled her into his arms, his mouth upon hers. He ran his slim, artist's fingers down the nape of her neck, earlobe giving her a rush of pleasure. The girl moaned his name, pulling him closer, and let her fingers run across the contours of his face in response. She felt nervous, excited, pleasured and heady, making her more allured. They knew what was to come the next moment. They wanted to rip their clothes, touch each other, caressing, moaning each other's names and make wild love. And that was exactly what they did. Though it was damn cold, the heat from their bodies was enough to light a fire. Avinash had always imagined the scent of her hair, but lying next to her, and breathing in its fragrance made him intoxicated. After making love, he ran his fingers through her semi-wet hair, wondering how close he'd been to her. What he had never told her was that he had fallen in love with her the first time he had seen her. Since then, he had hoped to meet her again and destiny had helped him. He felt the girl had similar feelings for him though she'd never expressed it. And now that she did, he felt ecstatic.

"You're beautiful," he murmured into her ears.

The girl closed her eyes and moved closer to him.

The night grew and so did their love. They were awed by the fact that they were lying in each other's arms.

It was an ecstatic feeling waking up with your soul-mate lying next to you. Avinash sat up on the bed and opened the window adjacent to it. It was late night and the drizzle stroked his face. The rain was still drumming upon the roof, sky gray with a waning crescent moon sheathed behind the black clouds. When he turned around, he saw the girl stirring under the blanket. After they made love, she had never left his room. They simply lay down in the bed, in each other's arms, and fell asleep.

Avinash hugged his knees and stared at her. She looked so beautiful, strands of hair spilling across her forehead, lashes winking at some dream, her half-naked body hidden under the blanket that was still warm from their lovemaking. He would have sat there watching her delighted until the light came. No wonder, he wanted to lock away the moment forever.

He slowly slipped from the bed, tiptoed across the dimly lit hall so as not to wake her up and fetched his sketch book. Lowering himself down on the floor, he drew her, outlining every contour of her face. He peered at it sensing something went amiss. It looked like a lovely sculpture, but with a significant, missing piece which would have made it spellbinding. Realizing what was missing, he circled his pencil in loops and coils until it was finished.

"It's perfect," he hissed under his breath, smiling, as he looked at the drawing, pride filled in his chest. He had drawn a picture of himself lying beside her, his head snuggled under the nook of her neck. He had drawn many couples earlier in the throes of passionate love, but depicting his own love and paying attention to every minute stroke raised heat in his cheeks as though their bodies merged together again.

Shoving the drawing back in to the sketch book, he thought he'd gift it to her on the day he'd propose to her. Perhaps then she'd write a beautiful poem on it and gift it back to him. Marvelling all those happy moments they were yet to share, he snuggled beside her again, pulling her close and fell asleep watching her. A streak of weak sunlight on his face slanting through the window woke him up the next morning. He stretched a lazy hand and fumbled to feel the warmth and comfort of the girl's presence. When his hand came into contact with an empty bed, he sat straight, eyes widened. There was no girl beside him. He kicked the blanket hastily off his feet, got down and darted across the room to find her, his heart ramming in his chest. But she wasn't there. And nor were her clothes in the bathroom where she had hung it on the clothesline to dry. It meant she had left without a word. He plopped down on the bed, his face sinking down with endless thoughts. What must have made her leave without a word: embarrassment, anger, or worse, regret? Before any negative feelings consumed him, his gaze fell upon a small piece of paper that sat on his folded clothes, the one he'd offered to her. He plucked the paper, his tense eyes running down the lines.

'Will meet soon' was written with a smiley next to it. Avinash heaved a sigh, tense replaced with delight. He picked up his clothes and breathed in the hypnotic perfume underneath his own. Now he understood why she hadn't woken him up in the morning. She hadn't wanted to disturb his sleep. He imagined how the girl must have stared at him, just the way he had and flushed with heat.

And the rest of the day was beautiful. The flowers bloomed. Sun played peek-a-boo behind the clouds. Raindrops left on the tips of leaves sparkled like diamonds. The birds chirped happily. In fact, every being on earth looked beautiful and happy. Or was it that Avinash felt so?

Replaying the previous night over and over in his mind, he felt both invigorated and shy. Suddenly his hands went still on the button he was fastening when a weird feeling crept in. What if something goes wrong? Something horribly wrong which he can do nothing about but stare at helplessly? What if their relationship is to be nipped in the bud? And things end bitterly between them?

He couldn't even imagine that. The very thought made his stomach twist in discomfort. When the girl had given her soul to him thinking he was the one, he swore to stand by her through thin and thick of her life, no matter what. He was not the kind of person who'd sleep with a girl just at the prime of receiving pleasures. He loved her with all his heart and soul and would continue to do so, no matter what. Besides, why would things end bitterly when they were madly in love with each other? Who would enter into their tightly formed relationship? She had left a note saying that she'd meet him and he trusted her.

He shook his head, brushing off his meaningless, stupid thoughts and went back to buttoning his shirt. Spoiled thoughts know how to make their way through someone who was in a happy mood. Today he was so happy and that was the reason why he had felt that way.

●

"Are you sure you're okay?" Avinash tried another time. He leant back on the wall, titled his head and looked over at Sahas carefully. He appeared tired and haggard. He'd come a week later to their room with a bulging bag pack filled with all his mother's love: Chettinad karapodi, rice appam, besan laddoos and many more of his all-time favourites, for she knew she wouldn't be seeing him for the next two months. The floor was strewed with luggage bags, his sandals right in the middle which he least bothered to put back in the shoe rack. Normally, Sahas would have already been in action, organizing them in their places. But he strangely looked different and neither had he spoken a single word. Not even a hug or a smile, Avinash thought, heaving a tired sigh. By now, he had got accustomed to his friend's unusual mood swings. Though he smelled something suspicious, he remained silent too. He flicked his wrist to check the time. It was getting late and he had to go to work. Dismissing his friend's quirky behaviour which he had been familiar with since childhood, he picked up his own bag and bike keys.

"Okay, I've got to go. Just call me if you need something," he pointed his finger to the north side indicating a new phone booth that had been installed just two blocks away from their room.

Yet there was no response. An embarrassing silence hung in the air.

When Avinash was just about to walk off, the silence broke.

"Avi, can you help me with something? I'm confused," Sahas sat up on the bed and hugged his knees, a lost puppy look in his eyes.

Avinash swivelled around, instantly picking up the anguished tone in his voice. Dropping his bag down on the floor, he walked up to Sahas and sat beside him, looking at him cautiously. "What's the matter?"

Sahas hesitated. "It's about Mom," Avinash felt worried, making wild guesses inside his head. Was it something about her health? Had his friend told her about his dad? Was she devastated by the news?

Sahas broke his chain of wild thoughts. "I don't know what has gotten into her lately. She says she's worried about me all the time. She thinks I have no one in my life to look after me." Avinash glanced over a hurt look at him by that implication. Wasn't he there for his friend? "No, she didn't mean that," Sahas shook his head, reading his friend's expression. "We are always there for each other. But later, you will have to choose your own career path and will have your own life. She has been saying stupid things like how I could live without her and that I needed someone—"

Avinash blinked in confusion. Why was his friend beating around the bush and not coming to the point? Every mother on earth would feel the same. What's so strange about that? And so he asked the same. Sahas bit his lip feeling stupid that he couldn't even articulate what was in his mind. He lowered his head, resting the chin on his knees, and took a deep breath. "She knew it's too soon, but for some reason, she wants me to get married," he finally forced the words. Avinash was so startled he jumped out of his skin. He burst out laughing, holding his stomach tightly. The next minute he was on the floor, tears leaking, unstoppable laugh consuming him."You, ma, ma... marriage?" He was too busy laughing he hadn't quite heard his friend say something else. "But I said no as I am looking for someone and sure will after we both get settled," Sahas yelled again, now grabbing his entire attention.

Avinash rooted to his spot on the floor, hands still on his stomach, mouth gaping open in shock. He stared at Sahas, blinking. "What did you just say?" He had no clue he looked like a shocked chimpanzee. "What do you mean looking for someone?" Had his friend just now hinted that he was looking for a girl? A GIRL... seriously? Not that he was a gay but how on earth could that be possible? He stood and looked down at Sahas. "What's cooking man?"

Sahas flicked his eyes, uncomfortable, like he was caught stealing. "I'm sorry Avi, I should have told you about this a long time ago, but I couldn't. Actually, I'm confused myself. I wasn't sure about this until Mom brought up the marriage question," he lowered his gaze, unable to meet his friend's.

Avinash was still staring at him, his mouth wide open like a large black hole. At least a black hole could swallow everything near it, but he couldn't absorb his friend's shocking revelations. How on earth could Sahas fall for a girl? He couldn't even dare to speak to a girl. Or even look at them properly, let alone speak. He was the most shy, reserved person Avinash had ever seen.

"I can't believe this," he plopped down on the bed, neither of them saying anything for a long time. "Whoah...okay," he clasped his hands with a sudden whoosh of excitement once he had recovered from the shock. "Details, I want specifics. And I want you to show her right now, my friend. Now that's your punishment."

Avinash knew nothing about the girl his friend was in love with. All he knew was that she belonged to the same college as Sahas.

"What does she look like man? Long hair with shaggy curls?" Avinash asked. He kept looking back over his shoulder asking Sahas choking questions. They were on the way towards Sahas's college to check on the girl and if possible have Avinash introduce him to her. Besides, all he could think of lately was long hair. He was so obsessed, and also, they hadn't spoken to each other since the night they'd made love. He thought he'd narrate his friend the whole story later and was sure that Sahas would never get the wrong impression.

"Why are you so curious?" Sahas's voice invaded his thoughts. "If you've ordered your dish, it will soon come to your table," he said, referring to Avinash's boundless curiosity.

"Just because you've ordered something doesn't mean you can't drool about it," Avinash grinned. "Besides, you have started to speak more intelligently since you fell in love, huh. The magic had already started its spell." He teased.

Sahas blushed from behind.

Avinash pulled up the bike right in front of the college's gate blocking the way. Haste and curiosity made him clumsy. They walked hurriedly past the familiar blocks. Sahas led him straight to their campus park saying she'd usually stroll or sit there at this hour.

Avinash found it amusing to learn that his shy friend had kept an eye on a girl's timetable. "You're a genius, man."

Not long after Sahas spotted her, they both dodged behind the trunk of a huge neem tree, enough to hide them both. Sahas's heart thumped in his ears, his palms clamped with nerves.

Avinash bore an exciting gaze. "Come on, where's she?" he asked impatiently.

Sahas heaved a sigh, his trembling finger stretched to a girl who was speaking to someone with her back facing them.

Avinash flicked his gaze into the line of his friend's direction excitedly. And something struck him, something strange, familiar like a connecting dream, like he knew the girl very well though she stood with her back towards him.

"There she is!" Sahas said, retreating his finger and went back to hiding behind a tree, blushing. "Her name is Aarti."

A flash of recognition shot through Avinash's eyes. He knew what was to come. His eyes flicked from the girl who had just turned around and then back to Sahas. Avinash's knees nearly buckled, mouth went dry. His heartbeat rose and so did his breathing. He had never realized that destiny would strike him such a blow.

Sahas dragged him behind the tree. "What do you think? Isn't she beautiful?" He breathed, still holding his friend's hand.

But Avinash didn't feel his hand on him. All he felt was numbing pain. A pain that was shocking and instantaneous, as if someone had neatly inserted a sharp blade into his heart. There she was, his girl, standing tall with her lovely long hair behind her. Yes, the girl he had fallen in love with at first sight, the one who admired his drawings like they were her own art, and the one he'd made love with and shared his soul with, picturing she'd be his life partner soon. She was Aarti, the long-haired girl of his dreams.

"Come on, tell me, isn't she beautiful?"

Avinash stared at him, eyes wide open, but said nothing. There were no tears either. He was still in shock. The tears would come later. His face mirrored his state of mind but Sahas was too occupied to realize his pain. If the characters had been switched, Avinash would have instantly picked up any changes in Sahas's expression. Not just an expert at reading emotions, but also hiding them. He swallowed a gasp and dropped down his gaze, heartbroken. How could words flow when every part of his body was broken to pieces? He excused himself and walked away from there, pulling his mobile from his pocket. He cradled the phone to his ear, implying he got a call. He pretended to speak for a few minutes, though he secretly dabbed at the tears shivering in his eyes and took a moment to regain his posture. A moment later, he walked back to Sahas hastily, head lowered. "I've got a call from the library, very urgent. I have to go," he said, not meeting his gaze.

Sahas stared at him puzzled. He had expected a long chat in their college canteen, all three of them. He was so happy and needed him desperately to share his joy, not realizing that it was his friend's nightmare. But he said nothing. Neither did he suspect anything fishy. He just believed that his friend had to go to work. "Okay Avi. We'll discuss… " he never finished as Avinash turned around pretending to make another call and walked away.

Destiny! Fate! Karma! Give it any name. But once it puts its cruel finger into someone's life and twirls it around for fun, the outcome is devastating, bringing utmost grief to people's lives. Just like it happened between two innocent friends!

Avinash was a perfect example of the above after learning about his friend's love. All his drawings were no more filled with lovely and spell-binding pictures. Instead, the white sheets looked as if they had been dipped in a bottle of black oil. He spent hours and hours doing that. What was he? A stupid, headless creature! But they say an artist would express his inner self on the sheet and that was what he felt. Black! An invisible colour he assumed would conceal plethora of pained emotions he was going through. What could he do apart from that? Blame destiny and god, like everyone did? But how wrong he was, alas! Nothing seemed to mend his broken heart. A week had elapsed and the sufferings he had piled inside his heart became so huge that he finally turned mum. He was not his real self. He had changed a lot. Where was his ease of manner, self-contained charm that dissolved mistakes by good humour? They all vanished into thin air, just like him. Most of the time, he either spent in the library doing nothing though he pretended to diligently work extra hours or shrank in to long silences finding himself in a deserted place. He reached home late at nights, hoping to escape facing his friend. He had no other choice. What would he say when his friend talked about Aarti and how much he loved her? The discussion would be painful. So either he held little communication or nothing. He couldn't even share a slice of his pain with Sahas, who would undoubtedly collapse if he learnt the bitter truth.

It was like Avinash was caught in a maze where there was no way out.

There had been no messages from Aarti. Perhaps she felt too embarrassed or too shy to call him and must be desperately waiting for his call. Now he clearly understood the dread that filled him the morning after he made love to her, the invisible fear that hovered over him making him feel so insecure.

But all the conflicting emotions were put to halt that morning when he saw his running shoes. When you can't face up to a sticky situation and feel that there is nothing left to do, all you can do is to run away from the problem. That was the best solution, at least for the time being, wasn't it? All those self-help books about being positive and brave when times were tough didn't seem practical. So, when one of his friends, a professor from his university, told him about a boring historical tour, boring to Avinash at least, he decided to join it. Wouldn't it be better than sitting in his room, listening to his friend telling him how much he loved his own girlfriend, or dreading his mobile ringing and assuming it to be Aarti? At least he could lick his wounds somewhere far away in peace.

"You never told me you're leaving for a tour," Sahas accused him blithely, sitting cross-legged on the bed looking like a petulant child.

Avinash didn't look up. His eyes were raw from crying all through the night for days and days, face looking gaunt for he had not eaten a decent meal since a week. He laid the suitcase on the bed and flipped it open.

"I mentioned it days before, you must have forgotten it," he said with his head down, feeling embarrassed by the way he looked.

Strangely, Sahas hadn't suspected anything fishy about his friend's weird behaviour. Perhaps he was too occupied in day dreaming.

"Maybe you're right," he said. "Do you think I look dreamy and moody these days?"

Avinash picked up his blue shirt and shoved it into the bag recklessly, pretending he hadn't heard.

Sahas heaved a sigh. "You are so busy Avi. You don't bother about my love. I'd shown Aarti to you days ago and you have not said a single word about her. What kind of a friend are you," he said with a pout.

Avinash's hand suddenly froze on his bag, his jaw tightened. He felt cold and shivered despite the sun being hot enough to make the pavements sizzle.

"What do you think? How does she look like? It's not wrong to fall in love, right?" Sahas shot questions like the balls being shot out from a tennis ball machine, giving the player no time to think.

Avinash's face went hot, throat parched. He hurried up shoving his clothes into the suitcase, implying that he had to hurry or else he'd miss his bus.

But his friend took no notice.

"I don't know Avi, I feel so terrified just looking at her. Deep inside, I have a thousand things to say to her, but when she walks up to me for a chat, I turn mute. I love her so much. But at the same time, I'm afraid. What do you think I should do? Please help me. You're my only friend in the world, aren't you?"

Avinash paused packing and looked up to stare at him for the first time. He didn't itch to, but maybe the genuine yearn in Sahas's voice made him do so. "When you love someone, you shouldn't be afraid. If you're afraid, then you should quit loving. Fear and love shouldn't be found in the same phrase, so never make that mistake," he said and they both locked their eyes for a moment, until a far distant cry of a child broke the spell. Avinash gulped, bowled by his own phrase. What had he said just now? Had he suggested that his friend propose to Aarti? But he never wanted that, right? Aarti had always been his girl, but the words had flowed out on their own. Or perhaps they were meant for him and had been spinning inside his head all the time.

"Wow Avi, you just spoke like a love guru," Sahas clapped, laughing at his own joke. And then suddenly everything made sense like he'd cracked the hard shell of a secret nut. He understood why his friend had been silent all these days. "You think there shouldn't be a third person in one's love life, right? If there is a third person, then there's a way for fear to walk inside and there would be a communication gap. Is that the reason you've been silent all these days?" Avinash swallowed hard, forcing a fake smile. He felt the noose tightening around his neck every minute. He had to leave. He couldn't stay there for a second longer.

"I have to go. We'll talk later," he forced the words around the lump that had lodged in his throat and left as soon as possible. Only after he climbed on his bike and past their lane, that he allowed himself to break into tears. For now, only his running shoes gave him solace.

Sahas was both excited and nervous the next morning, as it was a get-go day for his love. Last night, he had decided to convey his love to Aarti. His friend was so true in saying 'fear and love shouldn't be found in the same phrase'. He picked up his best clothes from the iron trunk. Crisp white cigarette pants paired with a black waist-length shirt. His mom had gifted them to him on his last birthday. Running his fingers tenderly over his attire, he recalled his mom's words. "You look as charming as a prince riding on a horse in these clothes beta," she'd said adoringly and had given him a kiss on his forehead.

Sahas felt nostalgic. He missed her a lot. But it was just a matter of few days, he thought, bouncing back to feeling excited. His mom would be so thrilled and happy to hear about his love. Later, he would take Aarti to meet her and no doubt she would love her as much as he did. Who could say no to such a sweet girl? And then they could all live happily together, except, he didn't want to settle in Bangalore. A place where his rival dad lived!

He hoped Aarti would take notice of him for he had always dressed casually to college, failing to capture the fancy of any girl.

In the college, Sahas felt burbled with nerves when he spotted Aarti strolling towards her block, her head hung low. He walked up to her, his heart thudding inside his chest and said 'hi' excitingly. She looked pale and drawn as though she had spent a week of sleepless nights.

"Are you ok, haven't seen you around much?" he asked.

She shrugged with a weak smile as response. Something wrong was written on her face, though he ignored. Summoning all the courage, he asked. "Would you like to join me for breakfast? I'm ravenous."

She nodded. They walked side by side silently to the college canteen. Though they had been there together myriad of times before, Sahas could feel the jitters in his body for the news he was about to drop on her. Besides, the canteen now would be filled with students and wasn't in fact, the right place for a chat. But he felt too embarrassed to talk to her in a more private area. They both sat at a corner table with ordered their respective dishes. As guessed, the canteen was thronging with students in groups who were laughing, clapping, speaking in loud voices and pulling each other's legs. But the mood between Sahas and Aarti was different. There was a taut silence between them with Aarti stirring her coffee listlessly, head lowered, the gesture that suggested either she was restless or bored. Sahas, on the other hand, struggled to look calm from outside, though inside he was all frantic, reciting the speech.

He kept stealing glances at her every now and then, wondering at her pointed silence. She wasn't looking like her normal self. Aarti had always been a lively girl who'd dissolve the embarrassing silence with her perky babble. In fact, she was the one who always took the initiative to talk to him. It was always her who'd say, 'Let's sit under that tree for a while or let's catch up for coffee.' But today, she looked lost and mum, like something terrible had happened. "So, where have you been all these day? Haven't seen you from a week or two?" Sahas broke the silence.

"Yeah, just had been down with little flu, I'm fine now though." She went back to stirring her coffee.

"Flu," he exclaimed, as though it was a dreadful disease. "How are you feeling now?" He almost got up from his seat to touch her forehead.

Aarti stared at him, puzzled. She knew him as the silent and shy guy in the group by far, but today, the extra friendliness he was showering upon her had taken her aback. "It's all right. I just had fever. But now I am doing well," she said flatly.

Sahas sat back on the table slapping him inside, embarrassed. "Oh! Did you go to the doctor then? I can accompany you if you want, you know," he added a moment later.

"No, I'll be fine," she cut him off, massaging her temples. "Can we not talk about it, please?" Sahas sensed a slight irritation in her voice. He'd never seen her so exhausted and drained. Her phrases were short and sharp. It didn't make sense to him. He hardly dared to speak any other word with the fear of screwing up everything, though that was what he'd done. Neither of them touched their breakfast, shrinking in to long silence. A moment later, Aarti rose and pushed back the chair. "I actually have lots of work, Sahas. I need to submit my thesis tomorrow. Can we talk later," she said, collecting her things from the table. Sahas stared at her, heartbroken. He felt like a loser who couldn't even grab a girl's attention with his words. Though he forced a polite smile outside, he died hundreds of times inside. Sahas didn't want to mess up her mood anymore.

"No problem, take care of yourself," he said in a low, disappointed voice.

"Thanks," Aarti said, picking her bag and left. Sahas sat back in the chair, his shoulders hunched, feeling like a pathetic loser. So much for thinking he would grab her attention with his clothes and speak his heart today. Let alone speak, he wasn't able to make her sit for a while. What was he: a stupid, small villager who couldn't even charm or amuse a city girl with his talks? He wished he had a scrape of charm Avinash possessed, who'd have spelled magic with his talk and set her mood. Feeling humiliated for the utter flop show, Sahas stood up to walk out leaving the untouched food on the table. No sooner as he turned around to leave than he saw Aarti walking back to him and his heart flinched. Did she forget something? He thought.

"Hey Sahas, I'm so sorry." She heaved a sigh, "Did I hurt you? I don't know what has gotten into me lately, but I am not that okay. Hope you didn't mind my company," she shrugged awkwardly, "How about breakfast tomorrow at the same time?" she asked. Sahas felt a sudden rush of fresh air. He nodded his head hesitantly.

"That's great," she clasped her hands. "Tomorrow same time for breakfast, okay?" She confirmed and bid a cheerful goodbye to him.

Miles away, the tourist bus was filled with the noisy chatter and laughter of students and professors. They all sat jumbled together, with the students sitting besides the professors and vice versa for once. They were heading back from the historical tour they had been on all week and everybody was in high spirits despite their exhausting trip, except for Avinash.

He was the only one who sat on an isolated seat in the back of the bus. And he looked as usual – devastated and broken. He had been like that the entire week. While his group had been savouring the pristine beauty of the historical monuments learning about their architecture, he sat alone either in the bus or on some isolated beach. If someone grabbed him, pulling him to the group, he'd simply say no. Or he'd preoccupy himself with the phone to spare any embarrassment or suspicion. Everyone wondered at his unusual behaviour. Wasn't he supposed to be the life of the tour? He was considered as the most jovial and energetic among their group. But here he was! Sitting all alone. "The tour is almost winding up. Come and join us in the front," a young, beautiful student with dark curls bouncing on her shoulders asked him for the third time. Who knew she might have had a huge crush on him? If it were earlier, he'd surely have flirted with her. But not right now; he was too broken-hearted to do so.

"I am fine here, please," he said in a low voice, avoiding any eye contact with her. The girl left upset that her favourite librarian's eyes were trickling down with tears. Thank god for putting off the lights inside the bus. He wiped the tears with the pads of his finger tips, wishing the bus would break down or take a long route to prolong the trip so that he could reach his place late. But nothing like that happened. Gone was the running time and now he had to face up the painful future, the very next morning. And now that he had also made a decision. The decision that was too painful to even think about for a second like a raw wound. He thought about it day and night, walking lonely on beach shores, staring at vast valleys surrounding the place, torn between love and friendship. Surprisingly, he had decided to step back. He preferred to lose his love to friendship. None of the options were easy, in fact. But he had to pick one. So he emotionally decided to back off and let Sahas and Aarti build up their relationship. He couldn't face his friend being a pathetic loser. Sahas's life had never had any harmony, Avinash thought woefully. His entire childhood had been filled with taunts and sneers from people around who used to torture him about his missing dad. Poor thing, he had to put up with so much, but he neither had the guts to confront them nor ask his mom about his dad. Sahas always used to stay silent, swallowing the pain, the only demeanour he learned through his life. It was only Avinash who knew how devastated he was from inside. Now, Avinash couldn't let that happen again and hurt him anymore But was he doing the right thing? Compromising on his feelings and backing off just because he didn't want to hurt his friend? Shouldn't he sit with Sahas and have an honest chat? Above all, shouldn't Aarti's feelings be taken into consideration? If he dug up all these questions, Avinash knew what he'd end up doing. Though he felt wrecked up beyond any repair, he tried to blank out all her memories. Tears flowed down his cheeks, and yet, the agony, the torture and the confusion were clearly seen in those tears.

It was a Sunday morning. The sun had shifted to the middle of the sky and beamed like a fierce ball that would scorch the entire city beneath it. With his friend about to reach home, Sahas was absorbed in his weekly routine of cleaning the house which he'd been meaning to do from so long. Coz once his friend reached home, he wouldn't be able to do anything. He pulled all the blankets and sheets off the bed and snapped them, beating, the dust. With a large broomstick in his hands, he worked on every nook and corner of the room that was covered in cobwebs. Amidst, he kept on thinking about Aarti. As promised, she had joined him for breakfast the other morning and they had had a long chat, though he never spoke about his feelings for her. With every passing day, his love for her kept enhancing. He sometimes sensed that something was troubling her. She often looked lost and deep in thought in the midst of their chat. He thought of asking her the reason several times, but thought better of it and kept mum. Sahas reached the wardrobe with the broomstick. There was a thick accumulation of dust on top, where his friend shoved his drawings. Sahas usually never cleaned that area because he always feared that some important drawing would get mislaid. But that day, looking at the cluttered, dusty objects, he couldn't hold back the impulse to clean it. Maybe destiny had decided so. He closed his eyes and swept up the dirt as bits of dust bunnies swirled and spilled on the floor. As he worked deep inside, there came down a few rolled drawings and fell on the floor which had been shielded from view by piles of some books. Biting his lip, he laid the broom aside and gathered the fallen drawings carefully to put them back in their places. He would never have peeped at them, not on a normal day, but one of the rolls was half-opened, prompting him to unroll it completely. When he did, he froze in his place, his knees buckled in shock.

He picked up the drawing in his trembling hands. In the drawing were Avinash and Aarti. They were on the bed, probably naked with their torsos covered under a single blanket. Avinash was caressing her long hair, kissing her forehead passionately. Aarti's head was lying on his bare chest as if it were a pillow. If someone looked at the drawing, there would have been a rush of heat churning in their bellies.

Sahas stood shell-shocked. He snapped his head away almost immediately, unable to look at the drawing any longer and collapsed on the floor. His breathing became heavy, and the blood flowed violently through his veins. He knew that his friend had that special talent of picturing someone and drawing without looking at them. It meant that Avinash had fantasized about him and Aarti. Sahas tightened his fist in fury, burning with wrath. How could he? How could his friend do that to him? How could he cheat on him? He knew how much Sahas loved her, didn't he? Sahas wracked with rage.

The drawing from his hands fell to the floor. Sahas didn't have the slightest clue that his eyes were betraying him. In that moment, his mind didn't allow him to predict his friend's well-known behaviour. All he believed was what lay ahead of him. In rage, he grabbed a glass lying nearby, over and over picturizing the image of Avinash and Aarti in bed, naked, making love and smashed the glass into smithereens. Shards of glass sliced through his palm sputtering beads of blood on the floor. But he felt no pain. His hands were numb. The mental pain overshadowed his physical pain.

When Avinash came back to his room after the tour, he was a little taken aback at the state of the house. The rooms were eerily silent and dark, with curtains drawn in. Sahas never liked it that way. He always wanted fresh sunlight slanting in through the windows. Avinash went to the kitchen and was stunned to see how cluttered it was. Part of it had piles of dirt as if the cleaning had been stalled in the middle. The dishes stank in the sink. He looked around but there was no sign of Sahas anywhere either. It meant he must be in the park. But Avinash felt too exhausted to go and look for him. He dropped his bag on the floor and plopped down on the bed, his legs and hands stretched out, feeling dead. Not long after he slipped into a short nap, muffled sounds woke him up. Rubbing his eyes, he sat up on the bed and peered in to the kitchen. It was Sahas tidying up the kitchen.

Avinash walked inside to tend himself a cup of tea. His head was throbbing with awful headache. Jerking his stiff neck back and forth, he stood against the tiny counter watching Sahas.

"Hi, I was asleep when you came in. I didn't notice you. I'm so tired after all that tour stuff. I badly need a tea man, else I'd collapse here," Avinash said.

But Sahas neither turned around, nor responded. Instead, he kept scrubbing away at the stain on the counter.

Avinash, too occupied with his headache to notice the change in his friend's behaviour, hadn't known that there was thunder hiding behind the silence. "You okay?" he asked, kneading his neck when his eyes suddenly caught the bandage on Sahas' left wrist. Straightaway, he pulled his hand into his and looked at the wound worryingly.

"What happened?" he enquired.

Sahas stood muted, balling his right fist at the side. Avinash quickly unwrapped the bandage, gob-smacked expression on his face at the sight of a raw scar on his palm. "How did this happen?"

"I'm fine, just leave me." Sahas muttered, trying to loosen the hold.

"No you're not." Avinash almost yelled holding his hand tight, completely blanking out about his own headache. "Look at the wound. It's so raw. You must have bled a lot."

Sahas stared up at Avinash, his jaw clenched. But what he witnessed wasn't the anxious face of a friend who was worried about his wound. Instead, he saw the drawing of him and his girlfriend on the bed, naked. His heart quaked with anger.

"It will be better if we go to the hospital. The cut is deep, and might need stitches." Avinash was engrossed in inspecting, clueless that it was the result of vicious jealousy.

Sahas suddenly yanked his hand back saying, "There's no need for it."

His friend could only see the virtual stains on his hands, but not his stained soul covered in gallons of betrayed blood. Sahas still couldn't believe that someone he considered not just his best friend but also his soulmate had deceived him. Now, it all made sense to him, why Avinash had remained silent whenever he fondly talked about his love for Aarti. His friend had been operating behind his back to gain the favours of Aarti. How could he?

"We should go to the hospital," Avinash repeated, not sensing the hint of anger on Sahas's face.

"I told you I am fine. Please leave me alone." Sahas snapped at the top of his voice.

His irritation flared up like damp firewood, yet he only showed a tinge of it. If he had shown the entire rage, Avinash probably would have been burnt to ashes.

And then, Sahas walked away, wearing a disgusting look.

Avinash froze, confused and distressed. He had never heard this piqued tone in his friend's voice before, not even when he was stressed. What had he done? Avinash thought miserably. He was already deep neck in pain and now his friend's rude behaviour pushed him on the verge of breaking into tears. Just then, his phone blared with a message. In fact, it had been ringing and blaring with messages from long though he hadn't been in a state to look at it. Gulping down the tears springing up in his eyes, Avinash pulled out his mobile from his pocket and peered at the messages.

The world around him shook. It was a message from Aarti, her first message since the last time they had met. She said that she was about to come to his house and wanted to check on what he was up to. Avinash's heart raced at the speed of a super fast train. Beads of sweat trickled down his forehead and his body quivered. He had to stop her, else he couldn't even imagine the disaster. His mind quickly raced up with excuses. Without a further thought, his fingers clicked on the phone promptly.

'I'm not at home. Please wait at the bus stop. Will soon come!'

Avinash let out a breath of brief relief, shoving his mobile into the pocket. At least he was able to stop her from coming home. His hands turned clamp at the prospect of meeting her. What should he do now?

Avinash silently slipped from his room, unnoticed by Sahas and walked to the nearby bus stop, where he had texted Aarti to wait for him. As he took tardy steps, a million thoughts ran through his head, wondering about what to talk and not. By the time he reached, she was waiting for him.

Avinash's breath caught at the sight of her.

There she was, the girl of his dreams. She sat on a bench with a thousand eager eyes darting to every corner of the road, hoping to find him. She looked so irresistibly beautiful that Avinash drew in a sharp breath. He stifled the urge to duck behind a random vehicle and steal glances for a while for he didn't know what fate was in store for him. The very thought of giving his piece of mind, the dreadful decision he'd made gave a sinking feeling in the pit of his stomach.

Aarti spotted him across the street and raised an anxious hand waving in the air in an attempt to catch his attention, not having the slightest clue that he had been staring at her for quite a while. Avinash signalled her to remain in the same place and that he would be coming up to her. A moment later, as he reached her, he felt his heart soar, the way it did every time he saw her. The bus stop was almost empty except for a small family standing a few feet away. No sooner had he dropped down beside her, he caught a whiff of perfume from her hair, making him distractedly crazy for a moment. He longed to run his artist's fingers through her wet hair that had been damp from a recent shower and smell it just the way he had done on the night they made love.

"So how have you been?" Aarti's voice broke the spell.

How stupid can your heart act sometimes? Avinash thought painfully, slapping his face mentally to even think that way.

"I'm good," he said airily and after a moment of silence, he added. "What are you here for?"

"To meet you and talk to you."

He couldn't help steal a glance from the corner of his eye. She'd put on some weight, face flushed with eyes full of hope, making it obvious how much she longed to see him.

"What is it you want to talk about?" He tried to sound ignorant, praying soundlessly she shouldn't bring the topic of that night.

"About the night we spent together," she said almost immediately, a little taken aback at his ignorant tone.

A shudder passed through his spine. He didn't know what to say. But irrespective of his fear, he tried to look cool by fiddling with his keys, hiding the tremble of his hands. "Oh, that night! I can totally understand that," he stuttered, willing to wind up the discussion even before it started and run away, the new way he'd discovered to solve his problems.

"Just understand?" Aarti teased, a rosy blush flooding her cheeks. She felt too shy to even look at him. Avinash stared at her, horrified. She was getting it entirely wrong.

"Did I say anything wrong?" she asked hesitantly at a frozen look on his face.

"No," he shook his head naturally only to feel moronic. What was happening to him? Why was he forgetting the reason he had come here.

Just then his mobile blared, interrupting their discussion. A local number flashed on the screen. He picked it up thankfully for he could devise on what to speak in the break.

"Who's this?" he said and paused listening to the other side, swallowing hard. "Actually, I'm busy right now. We'll talk once I reach home." He put back the phone, his hands trembling.

It was Sahas calling to know where he was. What Avinash hadn't had the slightest clue about was that he was sitting in a small tea shop behind the bus stand, burning with jealousy, spying from where he had a clear view of the entire scene.

"Are you okay?" Aarti asked.

Avinash nodded.

"So, I had been wondering why I never heard from you after that night, the night you know…"

"I feel sorry for that night Aarti. It was a mistake," he finally cut her off, sparing her the embarrassment. There, he said it. Perhaps the call from Sahas added fuel to his courage. Aarti had a melting sensation in her bones. She stared at him as though she hadn't quite heard him. These were certainly not the words she had expected to hear.

Perceiving the plethora of emotions pouring over her face, he added, "In fact, it should have never happened. You don't need to see me just because you slept with me. Just assume it was an unfortunate one-night stand. Frankly, it took me a week to come out of that loop and I suggest you do the same," he said coldly with an intent to break her heart for ever.

Each word he said had sliced his throat, but he was fabulous at suppressing his emotions and putting on a brash look of confidence.

Aarti's heart broke to pieces. "Unfortunate one-night stand?" she asked in disbelief. "I thought you loved me and so..." the words hung in the air as she felt too choked to even utter the words.

An uneasy truce hung in between them.

"But, it wasn't as if we had partied, got drunk and eventually jumped into bed. We did it knowingly, Avinash," she said, still holding a flicker of hope. How stupid she was. "And is that what you felt even when we were making love?"

Avinash looked away, sweat forming under his arms. "Oh, don't make a big deal out of it Aarti. Just because we had sex, it doesn't mean that we should get into a relationship and move forward." That stung! She was hurt. He called it sex and not 'making love'. For him, or for most men, it was always just sex, but not for her. They were a world apart. Making love was an emotional, intimate experience and brought about a sense of belonging. It was an expression of love. And till now she had thought he felt the same way. Though they had never said so, weren't they deeply in love? Didn't he feel the same way she felt even for a moment?

Avinash broke into her thoughts. "It's like living a lie all your life, Aarti. And I can't do that. I can't put on a mask and act. I want you to understand that," he said matter of factly, realizing that was what he was doing exactly that moment.

Aarti felt mortified by his mocking remarks. Her face turned pale with humiliation. Was she a fool to have believed he loved her? How easily had she fallen for him? What should she do now? Praise him for being so honest who had a great grip on his emotions, not giving her a false hope. She couldn't do that. Her upbringing wouldn't let to do so.

"You're being so unfair," she said, tears springing up in her eyes, "I loved you with blind devotion but it seems I turned out to be a fool. There's no point of explaining about what that night was to me to a person like you."

Avinash's heart clenched. There shouldn't be any crying, he made silent, thousand prayers, coz, he couldn't stifle his desire once he witnessed the tears in her eyes and perhaps would even pull her into his arms and apologize. "I'm sorry," he almost said to himself, "I didn't mean to hurt you."

"But you did," she cried.

She couldn't stay there for a minute longer. She was stupid to have even come this far for him. She must have ended this over the phone. What was the point of talking to a person who had never loved you and felt nothing for you? "I think I should leave," she forced the words through a lump and rose to her feet hastily, swallowing the tears. She couldn't give him the satisfaction that she was dying to be loved by him.

Avinash remained mum, looking away, implying that she was right. He stared at her helplessly as she marched away with heart broken, just as his was.

No sooner as she dragged herself away in deep hurt than she promptly froze in the middle of the road and looked back over her shoulder.

There were tears of despair in her eyes, screaming out for his adoration and attention. She couldn't leave just like that. Her experience with him wouldn't die until her last breath. It was like a treasure, because she loved him, and would, till her last breath. What should she do to make him understand that? She looked at him, her eyes pleading, screaming silently to call her back, hug her and console her as she wept on his shoulders, declaring that all that he had said was a lie and that he loved her as much as she did.

But nothing like that happened. Avinash stood like a statue, burying his emotions. He felt the earth should open and gobble him up. Conflicting emotions rattled within him. Pain, heartache, defeat and yet uncontrollable love! She came to him so longingly to hear some beautiful words and what had he done? Wasn't she the one whom he would love till his last breath? For a moment, he considered thrashing this emotional mess out calling her out, putting an end to it all at once.

But, he couldn't do it for his friend's sake. He was too stupid to realize that he would have to face Aarti in the future as Sahas' girlfriend. All the hopes and dreams of being with him were shattered to pieces as Aarti turned hopelessly around, feeling knots in her stomach. Before the feeling sank into her heart, something whooshed from behind, flinging her into the air with such a force that made her spin like a rag doll before thudding her body to the ground with a crunch. And everything in front of her eyes went dark. She no more felt anything.

Everything happened at a lighting speed. One moment Aarti was standing on the road, her pleading eyes looking at Avinash, and next, she was taken up in the air and soon thrashed on the ground. It was a bus thundered recklessly from nowhere that hit her. Or was it she who, lost in her own world, had missed the traffic light which had turned red for pedestrians?

A huge circle had formed around her, faces peering down anxiously at the girl whose body lay in the pool of her own blood, legs twisted in an impossible manner, eyes gouged out. Avinash was one among them who was staring at her, his face white. He had no track of when the ambulance had pulled up with a blaring siren, the paramedics rushing out and taking Aarti inside on a stretcher.

Someone shook his shoulder asking if he knew the girl, but Avinash could neither feel the touch nor hear him. He sat numb with shock beside Aarti who was lying on a stretcher under the blood-stained white blanket. She was fogging the oxygen mask that lay over her nose and mouth, gasping and struggling to breathe. Avinash stared at her as if he was having a nightmare and would soon wake up and realize that it was merely a dream.

As the ambulance pulled at the hospital, Aarti was rushed inside with Avinash frantically following them. He took her swaying, lifeless hand and squeezed, assuring her she'd be fine, though she wasn't in a state to recognize anything.

For the next hour or so, Avinash was caught up in a whirl of formalities, filling the details of Aarti in the form provided by the hospital staff, leaving his mind little space to think about what was happening. Or he'd frantically walk around the hallway, against the rules, murmuring over and over in shaking voice. 'She'll be fine, she'll be fine.' It was only after a white clad nurse approached him with blood-stained clothes and accessories of Aarti, that the shock subsided and panic seized him.

"She's fine, right?" he asked over and over. He imagined how she lay, almost lifeless with numerous tubes snaking out of her body, the beeping machine hooked up to her chest struggling not to go flat.

The nurse pulled him aside by his arm. "I already told you that you are not supposed to stand here. Please don't make me shout."

But Avinash said nothing. Instead, he looked at the glass door leading to the room, imagining bunch of doctors operating on Aarti. "You think she can feel the pain when they operate her?" Tears welled up in his eyes.

The nurse looked in his direction. "I know it's a hard time for you. Please don't panic. Did you inform her parents?"

Avinash shook his head and dropped his gaze. "It was my fault," he then whispered in a broken voice. He shook terribly from head to toe. "I caused the accident."

The nurse stared at him in bewilderment.

"Yes, it was me who asked her to wait at the bus stop. It was me who stood like the dead when she expected me to say those three magical words. It was me all the time. It was me who stared helplessly at her when she was smashed and tossed up in the air. It was me... I should have stopped her," the words poured out in a frenzied pace. He had no clue why he was saying all these to a stranger. Perhaps, he needed someone to blurt out his guilt.

A dense silence followed.

"I'm sorry," the nurse dabbed at her eyes. She imagined what the girl must have been to him. Though she had been witnessing myriads of such cases in the hospital, she felt a tug at her heart.

"She'll be fine. I'll pray for her." She pressed Aarti's gory clothes into his hands, patted his shoulder reassuring and left.

Collapsing down on the nearby chair, Avinash breathed in from the clothes the familiar perfume that had him spell-bound and broke down. Now that the shock had subsided, he cried bitterly, covering his face with Aarti's clothes until they turned damp.

When he finally walked up to the big reception area, he sank into a plush sofa, looking around. The room was filled with mixed faces, some joyful, celebrating the arrival of a new family member, others anguished and scared while they desperately waited for news of their loved ones, who were struggling to live. Avinash sadly thought he belonged to the latter category.

Resting his head on the pads of the sofa and staring blankly, he woefully thought that he should never have answered Aarti's message or met her. Perhaps, things would have been different then? What worst could have happened? Sahas would've come to know about the brutal shock and chaos would've ensued. So be it! In fact, Avinash was ready for that. He'd do anything to win his love, not even minding to beg his friend on his knees, if only Aarti could make it! The very thought brought shivers. He offered a million prayers to god under his breath for her speed recovery. Amidst all these thoughts, he suddenly froze at the sight of a person at distance. It was Sahas who had just dashed into the hospital with a frantic and worried look on his face as he pushed opened the door. Avinash would never forget that look on Sahas's face when he glanced up at him. It was a harrowing and piercing look that conveyed a thousand accusing words without uttering a single word. Avinash stood up hastily, his nerves racking with guilt. There was no reason for him to feel that way, but he just couldn't help it. Perhaps the way Sahas was shooting him disapproving glances that screamed 'offender' made him feel so? As Sahas approached, Avinash attempted to talk to him, though his mind went blank on what to say; poor thing was clueless he had been spied all along.

But Sahas jerked away, eyes brimming with tears and wrath. There, he had said it all without a single word. He swore under his breath that he wouldn't spare anyone, not even his friend, if something turned out wrong with Aarti. He then turned away, leaving Avinash alone, feeling miserable and cruel.

After what felt like ages, Aarti's parents reached the hospital. A passer-by had taken her ID card from her bag and informed them. This was the thing Avinash ought to have done, but he was too shell-shocked and blown away to think straight.

Aarti's mother was crying her lungs out, constantly wiping at her tears with her sari pallu. She held on to her husband who looked lanky, fit, yet broken and anxious. He had his arm around his wife's shoulder all the time. They were accompanied with a young guy, probably a relative, because Aarti was a single child. The guy looked strong enough to speak to the medical staff about Aarti. They were instructed to wait at the reception till a concerned person gave them the inside information. All three of them sat on the nearby couch spending anxious, endless hours with restless faces, waiting for someone to come and assure them that their daughter was doing well inside. A moment later, when a doctor emerged from the Medical Intensive Care Section where the most critically ill patients were being treated, Aarti's parents along with the guy, all hopeful of her condition went up to him. The doctor patiently spoke for a considerable amount of time with them on Aarti's condition, his hands making inexplicable circles in the air and his brow furrowed in anxiety. Just as he spoke, Aarti's mother cradled her head and sobbed into her husband's shoulder that shook uncontrollably with his own sob. It was such a brutal blow to them. The doctor patted the guy's shoulder saying something, probably the usual 'we'll try our best,' and left. The guy wrapped his arms around the heartbroken parents and led them to the couch where they all sat in stiff silence in tears.

Besides, what had the doctor said to them? Avinash wondered, panic spreading in his chest. Though he tried his best to be positive, he couldn't help the flicker of hope melting away, like ice on a hot pan. At once, he felt dizzy and suffocated. The familiar pungent smell of medicines hanging in the air nauseated him for the first time, forcing bile in his throat in fear. Swallowing it up, he rose and walked out from the closed walls. He had never been to a hospital before. Back in his village, there was only an old man who usually treated injuries with wild flowers and leaves. A moment later, Avinash found himself walking along the garden located far back of the hospital, beautifully landscaped. He tried to concentrate on the bright, vividly coloured flowers, hoping the sight would soothe his nerves. The breath of fragrant flowers and the living beauty of the surroundings convinced him that nothing could happen to Aarti, slowly rising up the waning hope. She would get well soon, come alive, perhaps succumbed with injuries from the hospital, Avinash pacified. It was just that destiny had put him to test. He swore he wouldn't hurt her this time, not in anyone's name. He'd tell her the truth and she had every right to know about it. He didn't know how long he had spent in the garden, walking around aimlessly, lost in thoughts. Only after he felt strong enough, he went inside the hospital hoping for some miraculous news. Just as he dashed opened the door, he came upon Sahas. Though Sahas gave him a cutting look, Avinash, deep inside craved for a hug and few soothing words, no matter what brash confidence he put on outside. For he knew that the confidence he was flaunting was a veneer of thin glass that was all shiny and glossy from outside, but fragile and could break even with a dull blow. But what was that rattling look on Sahas's face? He was swaying in his place as though a tranquilizer had been administered. Globs of tears were rolling down his cheeks. He took a few weak steps towards startled Avinash and then snatched his collar with such a force that they both jerked forward almost banging their foreheads. Their eyes locked in an awful silence. Avinash could sense Sahas's hand shaking around his collar in a very unsettling manner. Before an instinctive alarm set off in Avinash's head, Sahas loosened his grip as though he had no energy for the fight and left in tears without a word. Avinash stood shell-shocked. What did that mean? His mind went blank. Up to that point he held on the false hope tightly. But when he took weak steps towards the reception, his ears tickled at the screams from somewhere around the corner. At first, he had no clue whose screams they were, but as he headed towards the yells, his heart almost missed a beat, as the cries were calling out Aarti's name.

The world around Avinash spun as he stumbled towards the cries. All those hopes, his brash confidence and silent prayers shattered into pieces with every step he dragged himself on. As he neared the room, he realized they weren't just the screams of Aarti's parents. They were more like animal howls, crying, pleading, blaming god. Avinash sat outside, hugging his knees, hearing the unbearable voices until they subsided and someone pulled them out. Mustering all his leftover courage, he went inside, his heart ramming in his chest.

And that was it!

The sight of Aarti, lying lifeless on a white tray, her body wrapped in a plastic bag ready for the funeral pyre made him squeeze his eyes shut. Turning his face up at the ceiling, he let out a scream. A stream of tears poured out from both the eyes. When he looked back at Aarti, he saw her lovely, long hair had been shaved off. Her head was nothing but a round surface with blotch of scars. Back at the reception, the doctor had told her parents that she had suffered severe traumatic brain and permanent spinal cord injuries and she was almost brought dead. Avinash had not heard that or perhaps pretended that he hadn't. While he had been strolling in the garden hoping for some miracle, his girl took her last breath. And now she had completely vanished from his life.

What was he feeling right now? A pain, an excruciating pain as if someone had stabbed him a thousand times in every part of his body. Now that she could never be seen, touched or called out to again, Avinash's body convulsed. Without a warning, bile rose in his throat that he had suppressed earlier. He ran to a corner and puked violently, not bothering griming the place. He had never seen a dead body before and had never anticipated Aarti's to be the first one.

Wasn't this torment his handiwork? If only he'd said how much he'd loved or longed for her? Muttering sorry over and over, he collapsed on the floor, his body quaking in wrenching sobs, for a girl in a star.

They say communication is the key to a healthy relationship, but when it ebbs away between friends, the gap starts to grow. And so it was with Avinash and Sahas. Though they lived in the same house, the distance between them went vast and they rarely saw each other. And whenever they did, Sahas always snapped his head sideways and marched away, not knowing the real truth; he held his friend at fault. And if by chance their eyes met, Avinash saw fireballs of rage spitting from his eyes. It had been almost a month Aarti had passed away, but she still made her appearance tact between these two friends by making them rivals.

Avinash, on the other hand, felt hopeless and vulnerable. He knew that the two of them were going through the toughest and most awkward phase of their lives. Aarti had already given him a box full of darkness and left. Added to it, Sahas had stopped talking to him. At first, too occupied with his own anguish, Avinash ignored his friend's sudden taste for solitude. In fact, some relations might take their own course of time to restore as earlier, he told himself. But when the silence lasted for about days and went on to a month, he panicked. He wondered why his friend looked upon him as an enemy when he knew nothing about their affair. What had he done? Conflicting emotions ran in his head. Before an irreparable damage was done to their already strained relationship, he initiated a talk with Sahas. Not once, twice or thrice, but myriads of times. But every time, Sahas held his mouth in a tight seam, eyes averted; he left making Avinash feel miserable, lonely and confused.

Avinash wanted to shake his friend to make him break the silence and say something, but no, nothing worked. The room once so lively and perky had turned to a silent warzone.

It was an early evening when Sahas had just arrived home from his college. Avinash stood against the kitchen counter, waiting for his friend, determined to give his piece of mind to him. "Sahas, I'd like a talk with you," he said. And as usual, Sahas ignored him reaching for the tin off the shelf.

"Do you realize it has been a month you spoke to me?" Neither Avinash want to give up.

Sahas unfastened the tin, took some cookies, dumped them in a plate and went to the hall.

Avinash followed him. "See man, today I'm not letting you go silent. I wouldn't mind to lock the door and throw the key out, but I want to hear from you, that's it," he said exasperated.

Sahas paused, un-chewed food in the mouth. He gave Avinash a dirty look before snapping, "What is left to talk about?" The pile of dirty dishes in the sink, the untidy living room scattered with rolls of drawings had left him unmoved. But now, just the sight of Avinash and his voice brought a fire of irritation in him.

Avinash nodded. "Yes, it's true my friend, there isn't anything left. But we can't go on like this forever, can we? I want you to say something, anything, whatever is going on in your mind. Why are you silent and angry with me?" He demanded, not realizing that his voice was rising out of sheer impatience.

Sahas pushed the plate away, spilling the crumbles on the floor. "Angry?" he grunted matching his tone, "You want to know what I feel right now Avi," he looked into his eye, crushing the urge to slap his face, "dead, I feel like dead."

Avinash couldn't help a feeble, snappy smile. How could he make him understand that he felt the worse than that? Sahas had just lost a girl whom he had fallen in love with. But for Avinash, Aarti wasn't just a random girl. She was his love, his life, his everything.

"You know what the problem with you is, you only perceive things from one side, your side." He snapped, wishing Sahas could see things through his heart and not with his eyes for once.

And that snapped something in Sahas's heart too. He promptly rose to his feet and headed towards the door.

But surprising him, Avinash blocked the way with both his hands. He was so emotionally exhausted that he was determined to give him a piece of his mind and take one from him. It had to be a day of discussions that would put an end to all the misunderstandings between them.

"I understand you're going through the toughest phase and so am I, please I'm begging you we both sit and talk like grown-ups. Half the problem will be solved with an honest talk, you see." Avinash begged in his softest voice.

Sahas gave a scornful smile. How the hell could he understand what he was going through? Had he even realized how crushed and betrayed he was feeling right now? What he had done to him had been deceitful that even an enemy wouldn't think of doing. And he called himself his best friend. What irony! Sahas glared at him. And precisely the same moment, the drawing of Avinash and Aarti lying naked in bed and Aarti spinning in the air like a hapless pebble flashed in his eyes. A terrible fury crawled up his face.

"I don't want to talk to you," he said through gritted teeth. He then shoved Avinash recklessly aside and made his way towards the door. But Avinash wasn't giving up this time and he had no intention to either. So he marched towards him and held his arm in an attempt to stop him. But Sahas yanked his arm again and again and in the process, getting fed up, Avinash held his friend's collar.

"Your behaviour is killing me, Sahas," he yelled at the top of his lungs. "Can't you see that? Say something dammit, for the sake of our friendship. Stop this bloody silent treatment. Say something," he said, tears brimming in his eyes, the anguish of loosing Aarti and his friend's weird behaviour, everything squashing his heart at once.

Sahas stopped yanking his arm; instead, he glared at Avinash with a hateful look. Their eyes locked, lingered over in a tense silence before Avinash dropped his gaze down, his face closed. No, this wasn't the way he wanted things to go. He loosened his grip around Sahas's collar.

"I'm sorry Sahas. I don't know what has gotten into me," he said in a low voice.

After taking few quick steps, Sahas stopped at the doorway, perhaps for the sake of years of their friendship and spun around. Rage and jealousy filled his eyes like burning charcoal which outweighed his love for his friend. The words he'd rehearsed every day and night spun around his head once again. 'You failed to consider my sensitive feelings for my love. I believed in you so much and respected you for what you are, but what have you given me back, betrayal and infidelity? Perhaps, and only perhaps, I would have forgiven you if you had been brutally honest with me, and at least told me that you had sexual feelings for the girl with whom I was madly in love with. Though that would have crushed me, I'd have felt that my friend was being honest with me. But you cheated on me behind my back, trying to draw favours of Aarti. It's easier to forgive an enemy than a friend, Avinash.' Sahas blinked. Those were the words and feelings bubbling inside him, but he kept silent, like always. If he had said them out loud, they would at least have bridged the gap and misunderstanding. "I know what has gotten into you," he said sharply instead, "The lust! You know what Avi, sometimes I wish you had died in that accident," he added coldly before giving the door a loud slam on his way out.

The sour words flew like a pierced sword and stabbed Avinash's heart. He stood there speechless, his face going hot.

Bangalore was a city of ghosts for Sahas. He couldn't imagine his life here anymore. On the first hand, he had never wanted to come here because of his bloody father. If it wasn't for Avinash who'd stopped him with his faux concern, Sahas would have left the very day he'd come across Dayanand. On the other hand, he should never have met Aarti. The encounter with her was like chancing upon a raindrop on a sloppy window that vanished as quickly as it appeared, though he told himself, he'd have lived hundreds of years with her single encounter. And then came the worst part of betrayal by his friend. With every passing day, the anger and resentment kept swelling like an uncontrollable tumour. Now, he had too much on his plate to cope with. Forget about the college, he desperately wanted to go back to his village and mom. He'd work as anything there. In fact, it'd feel like heaven to help his mom in the small hotel she ran. Although they learned very little, they'd enjoy being together. But here it was a living hell, like an orphan casted away by his family.

One day, he decided to call his mother for he hadn't spoken to her in a long time, engrossed in his own melancholy.

He went to the local phone booth and dialled his village number. He waited for few minutes and then called back hoping his mother would have reached the booth by then.

"Hi," Sahas said, finding his voice chirpy to himself after ages for he believed the sound of his mother had the magic power to heal his wounds.

"Hello beta, how are you?" Sahas frowned, looking at the receiver confused. "Baba?" he asked, wondering why he'd taken the call. "I'm fine, Baba, how are you?"

"I'm fine Sahas beta. It's been long you've made a call with your updates. How is your college and studies?" he asked.

Sahas faltered before faking about his studies that they were going very well. The fact was he hadn't opened his books for ages. "Where is Mom, by the way?" he asked a little cautious, glancing at his watch. Baba usually left the hotel at about seven and would only return the next morning. He had never stayed at Sahas's house even though his mother had insisted that he should since he had no family and lived alone. Now it was half past nine and it seemed strange that he should attend a call at this odd hour.

"Sahas beta, I'm staying at your home from the last couple of days," he said.

Sahas's face lit up with a huge smile. The idea of Baba and his mother together welcoming him back felt good. He knew that Baba was in his seventies and that it was getting difficult for him to stay on his own.

"That sounds good Baba. In fact, I've always wanted that. Amma would have been very happy with your decision," he said warmly.

There came a pause. "Sahas beta, I've been wanting to call you for many days," Baba said slowly as though he was choosing every word with utter care. For some reason, Sahas's heart thumped lightly. "I was thinking it'd be nice if you were here." Baba added in an anxious voice.

Sahas's pulse quickened. "Why? Is everything all right?" he asked urgently, his stomach lurched.

And there came another pause as he stilled his breath to listen to the answer.

"It's about your mother," Baba's voice had an edge. "She hasn't been so well. It would be nice if you could come here and stay for a few days."

Sahas had not realized that he was holding the phone so tightly in his fist, his breath caught in fear.

"She didn't want me to tell you this though. She was afraid she'll disturb your studies. I've been meaning to call you by myself and now that you called, I thought you'd every right to

know about things. But don't worry beta, I'll take care of her…."
Baba went on.

Sahas pursed his lips, never actually listening to the rest of
the talk. His thoughts drifted to his mother, him visualizing her
on a rickety bed, sick and miserable, wanting to see her son and
yet suppressing the urge, not intending to upset him or disturb
his studies.

A stab of guilt pierced through him. He was so engrossed
in his own anguish that he had forgotten a poor soul had been
waiting for him in a village. The very thought made him unsteady.
Sahas hung down the phone and heaved a deep sigh. The next
second he made a decision to travel to his village.

Avinash creaked open the door of his room and stepped inside. It was dark and silent like a graveyard. There was nothing left here anymore. It had been two months since he had spoken to Sahas. Once, both the friends lived in the same poky room without minding each other's presence. But now, whenever they were together, it was like they were living in a house of burning charcoal. Besides, ever since their heated argument when Sahas had hurt him with his bitter words, Avinash had only seen him twice. He wasn't sure if Sahas was still living here or had left to his village for no more of his luggage could be spotted. Their relationship had turned so sour that the best friends had started behaving like sworn enemies, all in the name of a girl who wasn't on earth anymore.

Initially, Avinash thought that time would eventually lessen the tensions; often it was the solution to all the problems. But as days turned to months, he was tired of pleading, tired of running on a treadmill of misunderstandings. He didn't have any patience left to make peace with his friend. In fact, Avinash didn't go to work properly, didn't sleep well and hardly ate. His own existence remained torturous. Apparently, he'd discovered a sudden taste for solitude.

He lay on the tiny balcony on his back, his hands clutched beneath his head, sheets of drawings strewn across around. It was freezing cold as if he was sleeping on slabs of ice. Listening to the breeze flowing through the trees, he sadly recalled the days when the same balcony was filled with the giggling chatter of friends as they sat, eating and drinking contentedly. Sahas would cook a delicious meal for Avinash while he'd be engrossed in his world of art.

The wind picked up its pace, rolling and ending one of the drawing papers on Avinash's face. He took the fluttering drawing to his hands and gazed at it. It was Aarti's sketch, the one he drew her in the park. It looked so real, as if she was looking at him from the paper with her chocolate-like eyes. Avinash brought his face up close, trying to breathe in the fragrance of her hair.

What irony! When she was around yearning for his love, he had pretended to ignore her. But now, he was wishing she would come alive from the sketch and hug him.

Putting the drawing on his chest, he gazed up at the sky watching clouds floating above and then his eyes rested upon one of the brightest star. It looked beautiful and immortal. He wondered if Aarti had reached one of those stars shining brightly with the power of a beautiful soul in it. He envisioned her smiling face, the way she tilted her head and listened to him as though nothing in the world ever existed except him, everything flashed in the star.

A flood of memories swamped his eyes. He couldn't stop recalling how he had met her and how his life had changed since then. But the most grieving part was that she'd left without saying goodbye and he had to learn to live with it. He wished for a time machine where he could travel back and let her know his deepest secret, his unfathomable love for her.

It's true that sometimes one will never know the true value of a moment until it becomes a memory. Tears stung his eyes. What kind of life was he living? His best friend treated him like a sworn enemy. The girl he loved had vanished from his life forever. Sobbing, he held his head tightly, feeling an excruciating pain.

And then something occurred to him.

A drawing! There was the drawing he had done of Aarti and himself on the night he had made love to her, thinking it would be his gift to her. But when Sahas had told his story, his entire world had turned upside down that he totally forgot about it. It was his last memory of Aarti. Where did he put it? Avinash racked his brain, trying to recall. Yes, he had shoved it on top of the wardrobe.

He hastily rose and hurried inside to fetch it. Bringing the ladder from the kitchen, he climbed on it and rifled through the catalogues, pushing aside other things that might be shielding it from view. But he didn't find it. This was the place he clearly recalled putting it that night. Where it had gone, he wondered getting down the ladder. He then frantically searched every nook and corner of his house. In frustration, he pulled, kicked at the little furniture the room contained. But still, he couldn't find it. Disappointed, he collapsed on the bed. It was his last memory of Aarti, the times when they were happy. At least, gazing at it would bring the tiniest of comfort, like a pail of water in the desert, which he needed now. But there was no way it could have been misplaced, he thought hard. And then something struck him suddenly, something that had never occurred to him before! And everything made sense with an inevitability of thunder following the lightning.

Had Sahas chanced upon the drawing?

Sahas sat by a grubby window seat, his head resting against it, and watched the blurred landscape outside. He set off on an overcast morning to his village. As the bus sped past the familiar localities, his thoughts inadvertently took a trip down the memory lane. Memories of his childhood that was as unfathomable and deep like Mariana Trench flashed across his eyes. Avinash and him taking rides on the windy roads, screaming 'whooo' in excitement. With the roads in his village often slippery due to constant downpours, it was always Avinash who rode the cycle while Sahas sat on the frame. He was too frightened to ride while his friend rode at full speed around the hairpin turns, skidding every once and then with them giggling endlessly.

Damn all those memories, Sahas bit his lip.

The bus pulled up at the old Anjaneya temple as Sahas got down. He walked past the village men who were chopping wood, their faces flushed in cold. Sahas thought sadly how he had left his village with dreams in his heart, vowing to bring joy to his mother with his success who had worked hard day and night. Now what was he left with to show her except the emptiness and pain of a loser?

At the front yard of his house, he was greeted by Baba who was seen squatting by a cooking pot. It took a while for the old man to recognize it was Sahas approaching him as he smiled tiredly and hugged him, feeling relieved. Sahas made his way inside the small mud house with cracked walls with Baba behind him.

There she was!

Sahas's mom lay on the rope bed in the tiny, single room, that served as a sleeping area as well. She was just skin and bones and looked so weak and fragile. Sahas stood speechless, his heart sinking to his stomach. He dropped the luggage on the floor, took a deep breath, steeling himself before he sat beside her. The last time he had seen her, she had been hale and hearty, but now, it took tremendous struggle to utter even a few words or to turn from side to side.

Though every part of her screamed weak, her eyes shone with joy at the sight of her son. "How are you?" she said in a sluggish manner.

Sahas nodded silently, furious with her for not letting him know about her condition. He had thought it was a minor illness, but seeing her in this tormented state nearly killed him.

The woman lifted her trembling hands to his face and stroked gently. "Sorry, I've ruined your studies."

Sahas swallowed the tears pushing up to his eyes. Mothers! Poor things on earth, every minute they breathe, work, struggling hard, only to keep their children at comfort. But when they needed them at their low spirits, they swallow their loneliness, fearing to hurt their children and lead the rest of life in pain.

A stab of guilt thrust into Sahas's heart. He looked up at Baba. "What happened?" he asked.

Baba shrugged. He himself looked so weak and wrinkled that a terrible guilt engulfed Sahas. A grown-up kid had to take care of his parents when they grew older, but he had buried himself in the misery of his own problems and had not bothered about the people who loved him. Now after looking at this, he made a firm decision, a decision that might not be approved by his mother. But he didn't care anymore.

He leant down, steeling not to break down and spoke slowly. "Enough amma, now that I am here, I'm not leaving you anymore, not in this condition," the woman opened her mouth to protest, but he put a finger on her lips, his head shaking, "Only I get to talk. All these years, I listened to you. Now you've got to listen to me. I'm not going anywhere, you understand. I'm going to be here and take care of you. You see, you'll bounce back to your normal healthy life. Until then, I am not leaving your side."

He kissed her brow and looked into her eyes. A tear swelled at the edge of her eye before they drifted shut. Soon, she went into a deep slumber.

Sahas finally put a halt to his own dejected life and devoted his entire time to taking care of his ailing mother and the hotel. He took her to the nearby hospital and kept the treatment on for her. He woke up early in the morning, did all the household chores – sweeping the floors, cleaning the utensils, shopping for groceries necessary to run the hotel. He'd then clean his mother up with a wet sponge, filling in the details of his daily chores, the way she used to do when he was a child and had fallen sick and then he'd feed her. In the evenings, he became a common sight, crouching beside the line of village women, washing the laundry.

With his good culinary skills and little assistance from Baba, they soon re-opened the closed hotel, eventually running it smoothly. Sahas was overwhelmed with gratitude for the help Baba lent despite his elderly condition. Days passed as Sahas tirelessly worked for his family and the hotel. Soon, his mother recovered from illness and looked much better, or they all thought so. Somehow having her get back from feeble state to normal, Sahas found a little peace. With every passing day, as his mother healed, his own wounds cured as well, or were they buried under a temporary scar that was still raw. But truthfully, he rarely recalled about Aarti or Avinash. Whenever his mother would ask about Avinash, Sahas would keep tight-lipped or say brief words, not meeting her eyes. He hadn't had the heart to tell her about what happened.

But some days, the routines took dark side too. The woman would suddenly turn pale and drawn, her breath ragged, eyes distorted and soon she'd break into coughing spells. Sahas would panic, clueless what to do. He'd run and bring the local doctor who'd treat her with some leaves and then she'd return to normal, giving Sahas a breath of relief.

One cloudy morning, he walked to her with a bowl of vegetable soup. Putting his arms around her, he made her sit up, propping her back against a pillow and fed her.

The woman swallowed the soup silently. Between sips, she looked up at Sahas. "It's like you are my parent and I am your daughter."

They smiled at each other. Sahas recalled the sleepless night she'd spent taking care of him as a kid. She was very strong built back then who would lift off the massive cooking pot with no difficulty.

"Yeah, there's a role reversal. And if you don't listen to me, I will twist your ear," he teased.

She smiled weakly. "Sahas, don't you think you're tiring yourself too much. Juggling between all these works?"

"Of course not. In fact, I have become more rugged and handsome than before," he winked at her showing her his muscle. "I know you won't believe me. You can ask our neighbours. Now that I am good at all household chores, our village aunties are dying to give their daughter's hand to me."

The woman grinned slurping the soup. "How about your college then?"

"I already told you I wouldn't leave your side until you recovered totally."

"But the college…"

"Can we not talk about it amma, please?" he said, cutting her off. Watching her frown, he added. "Don't worry about me. I'm perfectly happy doing these things. I'll nurse you and make you run behind me and only then I'll leave." This was where he had to be, not somewhere far away.

When he finished feeding, she said. "I need to talk to you Sahas."

He wiped the soup stains off her lips and was just about to rise. "What is it about?" he asked nonchalantly.

"Not like this, bring me another pillow to support my lower body. Yeah. Now it's better. Thank you, my son. I've been meaning to talk to you from so long about this." She spoke in a low, urgent murmur.

Sahas tipped his gaze down at her and something in her eyes alerted him. Over the years, he had got familiar with that look, the look which said it was going to disclose something terrible or unpleasant. For some reason he dreaded the coming conversation.

"What is it about?" he now asked little cautiously.

The woman took a long time, perhaps steeling herself before she spoke. "You know Sahas, I have always been a fulfilled woman with no regrets, and at least I thought so. I was proud of the choices I made in my life. When you were born, people muttered all kinds of things when I walked past them. But I never flinched. I went ahead like weathering through a fierce wave. But still there were days when I dreaded if I could bring you up single-handedly or not, storming the insults without any support. But I did, you see," she smiled weakly with pride.

Sahas was startled for his mom never spoke to him this plainly. It would be an insult if he pretended knowing the plight she underwent. He was both embarrassed and sad though he hadn't shown it on his face. And he also knew many more were to come which he might not be ready for.

"But there were days when I had dissatisfaction for I raised you with a lie, a mask. Yes, I lied to you Sahas," she was staring off in to distance, her eyes painful. "I lied that your father died. No, he was all healthy and alive."

There was a brief pause.

"I know," Sahas muttered.

She held his gaze, and to his surprise, she hadn't registered any astonishment. "Baba, isn't it?"

He nodded.

She peeled her gaze off him, "But you don't know that I sent you to Bangalore with a motive, to make you meet your father, and of course, to make you pursue your studies."

Sahas stared at his mother in disbelief.

Though she wouldn't see him, she knew that look – confused, nervous, easily startled and quick to make judgments. The one that brought shivers to her for the inability of his son who couldn't cope with few revelations. But this wasn't the way she imagined to drop the news. She thought she'd take him for a stroll around a quiet place and then would speak her mind. But destiny had left her bedridden, leaving her no choice.

"I had been meeting your father for the last couple of months without your knowledge. In fact, he had been coming to meet me for many years, though I was rigid, declining to meet him in the start. But then I resigned, perhaps for the sake of his loneliness, or for you, or for myself. I'm not ashamed to say that I loved him, truly from the heart."

There was wetness in her eyes. Her face looked old with sunken temples, hollow eyes, and above all, a tired soul.

Sahas looked diminished, something valuable stripped away from him.

"I know how difficult it must be for you to stomach this news. All these days, I hid it from you, fearing you'd hate me,"

"I would never hate you," Sahas whispered back, but she didn't seem to listen,

"But now that I am dying, I made a decision. I no more want to have any secrets with you," she looked at her chipped nails, avoiding his gaze. "Sahas, I've been thinking you should stay with your…" Sahas wanted her to stop, wanted to scream 'shut up' and ask what she'd like for lunch or dinner or talk anything else, but it was too late, "father," she said through numb limps.

Sahas went blank in the face, air whooshed out of him. He stared at her in disbelief. "What did you just say?" his voice was hardly above a whisper. "Did you just say I should live with the person I've hated all my life?" He was furious to even think that way. "How could you even address him as my father? Where was this father when children mocked me about his whereabouts, where was he when people muttered all things behind our back, where was he when it was to teach me moral principles?" He uttered every word with great distaste.

A dense silence followed them.

The woman splayed her hand across and squeezed her son's hand gently. "I wouldn't blame you if you hate me for the decision. You've every right for it. But trust me, this is all for good. I hate to ask you this," she stirred uncomfortably breaking into a long, coughing spell, "But it would be my last wish, please Sahas. I couldn't ask you for anything else."

"No!" He yelled at the top of his lungs, yanking his hand away and stood. How could she suggest that? Had she gone mad? Amidst this, the word 'dying' slipped out of his mind. He felt suffocated in the house. He wanted to run away, but stood there leaning against the sooty wall, furious, pleading, negotiating, begging and denying. He had no track of how long they both argued back and forth.

At last he grew so tiresome, he said through gritted teeth. "He's always a dead man to me amma, just as you said when I was a child, that's it. You might forgive him, but I would never. And if you once again bring the topic. I swear I'm gonna kill you."

There was finality in his voice. And then he marched away with his mother pleading and crying from behind, "Please come back Sahas, don't leave me. I need you to listen to me." And he never got to hear the rumbling sound of his mother who coughed her lungs out shouting for him.

He silently marched to the nearby waterfalls, his entire world entangled in a web of secrets. He sat on a rock, his legs lowered into a small puddle underneath, motionless, watching the waters streaming down from the hills faraway. He hadn't yet recovered from Aarti's sudden death and his friend's betrayal and now this. It was like standing on a road and being hit by the same car over and over again – betrayal. He was furious with his mother for planting such a horrible idea in to his mind. He sat there for a long while, lost in his thoughts, watching tourists crouching in front of their cameras, smiling, women washing laundry, bunch of boys playing in the waters. It was the same place where Avinash and he had once spent myriads of times together. They used to stand under the gush of water for hours, drenching, shouting, pushing each other, playing until Sahas's mom took them home twisting their ears.

Sahas felt a knot in his stomach. His mother had worked hard her entire life without any genuine support from anyone, only to see her son happy. He couldn't reconcile how she had transformed in the last few days. It was the illness, and restlessness perhaps which had made her to blurt out such things. He would talk to her once she bounced back to her normal health. Till then, he'd pretend they never had this discussion. He realized he had been out for hours. It was nearly evening, the setting sun hiding behind the clouds. The image of his mother alone on the bed, crying, waiting for him to come back made him flinch. As he made his way back to his house, the anger diminished.

It was eerily silent and dark inside his mud house when Sahas returned home. Shame washed over him for leaving his mom this long alone. He could hear silent sobs from inside. He experienced a tight knot in his belly. The knot tightened with every step he took towards his weeping mother. He was wrong. It wasn't the sobs of his mother. It was Baba on the floor, sobbing, his head covered in his hands. Dreading, Sahas bent down to touch Baba, "What happe…" before Sahas finished, his gaze caught his mother and the words died in his mouth. Her face had turned white and stiff, her torso covered in an old blanket.

"She has left us Sahas, she has left us!" Baba hollered, pounding his face with fists.

Sahas froze in his place, speechless. And then there was silence, an intense silence with no noise at all, except for the thudding of clothes hitting against a hard rock in the distance, echoing the sounds of his heartbeat.

A slab of early morning rays through pulled curtains fell on Sahas's face. He lay on bed, not willing to drag himself out. Neither had he wished to be here, on the king size bed. It was like sleeping on a bed of hot charcoal. After what felt like ages, he pulled the curtains open off the large glass window overlooking a sprawling lawn. The morning dew had settled on the mowed grass. The garden was filled with all coloured flowers with graceful lanterns standing between them. The large pool in the corner where one could have a delightful dip at any time with the tiny fountain spraying sparkling colours beside looked breathtaking.

He had been living in this house for two weeks, but had never noticed how beautiful it was. Not that he wished to either. Living here was just a compromise he had made to fulfil his mother's last wish. It was Dayanad's house, not his. And Dayanand was only his mother's husband and not his father. His mother could have forgiven him and might have carried secret love for him. But for Sahas, he was hard-hearted and a selfish-wolf who had abandoned them and ran away for his own well-being.

Sahas counted every day, every minute and second ticking away here like he'd been living in a haunted house bewitched with voodoo. But in one way, the large dimensions of the house provided an escape to him. Dayanand and Sahas rarely surpassed each other, but when they did, Sahas would snap his eyes away, hastening his walk. Besides, Dayanand was forever busy travelling around and would be a rare sight at the house. But it was in the late evenings sometimes he'd have significant people come over. They'd all sit by the fireplace, sipping whiskeys and speak in loud volumes about business, politics and many other things. Despite all the doors and curtains shut, Sahas could overhear them from downstairs with him ignoring, his eyes squeezed shut forcing sleep. But it'd be impossible not to dismiss Dayanand's voice. Fragments of his bewitching voice, the one that had the power to absorb attention, drawing everyone into his vortex, would drift from downstairs. Sahas would picture him sitting by the fireplace, a whiskey in one hand, cigarette tapping into china in another, talking business between sips, with all eyes on him.

On some days, when Sahas couldn't endure the overstuffed luxury and comfort and felt nostalgic vibes longing for his low ceilinged mud house closed by sooty walls and mostly the simple rituals of having breakfast with his mother, he'd walk out of Dayanand's house. He'd go for long, aimless walks, wait until the sky turned dark and would sleep under some bridge amid beggars, filth around. He'd think about the pathetic fate he was showered upon by his own clan. He'd urge to run away, somewhere far from all this, but the promise he never made to his deceased mother would spring up like a gust of wind and make him bound hostage.

But he told himself that one day would soon come, the day when he'd wake up before dawn and walk out of the house, out of the luxury, out of Dayanad's life forever.

And surprising Sahas, the late night meetings had come to an end subsequently. After quickly freshening up, Sahas got down, ready to leave for college. When he was about to exit, a voice from behind stopped him. He was the male servant, in his sixties with a frail figure and thinning hair. He cooked, took care of the entire house and bossed the other servants.

"Sahas, you didn't have your breakfast even today," he reminded gently.

For the past two weeks, Sahas had been having his food outside. Or sometimes, he'd starve till evening, or worse, next day. But he wouldn't touch a thing on the table. "I'm actually running late. I have a special class. I'll have something at my college canteen," Sahas said and swung around.

"This is what you have been telling me every day," the servant's voice stopped him. "Look Sahas beta, your exams are near. Walking away with an empty stomach isn't good for you. I've made a special vada for you. You should taste it," he said with genuine warmth in his voice.

Somehow, the gentleness in his voice reminded him of Baba. Sahas recalled how defeated and sad Baba was when his mom died. He had cried his lungs out and begged him to fulfil her last wish. It was he who had pushed him here, despite Sahas's protests, and since then he had never spoken to him. The servant chirped in breaking his thoughts. "What are you thinking Sahas? Are you worried that it won't be tasty? Don't worry, I am a good cook," he smiled, gesturing Sahas towards a chair he had pulled out. For some reason, Sahas gave up being stubborn. He realized the old man acted more like a father than a servant.

Sahas sat around the antique dining table occupied with classy kitchenware. A massive chandelier hung from above, overlooking the table. He was served vada and coconut chutney on a fine china plate with varied forks and spoons beside he'd never seen before. Pushing them aside, Sahas nibbled at his breakfast with his hands. The old man went inside the kitchen to bring him some coffee. Just as he was about to finish, Sahas heard a voice drifting from upstairs. His head automatically snapped up, un-chewed food in the mouth, hand froze in mid-air. "A deal is a deal, no matter what. And we also need to ensure that we secure that client," Dayanand spoke on his cell phone, his voice sharp and strident. It was just about eight in the morning and the man descended the steps in an expensive, pin-striped suit, already starting about the day. Sahas couldn't help steal a glance at him who was walking with his chin raised up and shoulder blades pulled in; perhaps giving shudders to the person he was talking to. He looked as confident and professional as Warren Buffet.

Sahas gave an involuntary shudder too hating to let someone create turbulence in him, especially this man. "Well Shyam, I'll be at the office in a few minutes. We can have the discussion there," Dayanand said, his eyes fixed on his son. Snapping the mobile shut, he walked towards Sahas and stood beside his chair. "How did you like the breakfast?" he asked casually, as though they were sharing the intimacy of son and father.

Sahas peered down at his plate, his body inadvertently slumping like a broken tree. He was in no mood to share any culinary conversations. Neither was he hungry anymore. He hastily launched into finishing the breakfast, intending to get the hell out of here as early as possible. But Dayanand stood there, staring down anxiously, hoping for a response. In fact, he had been trying hard to have a chat since the day his son had stepped into the house. But all his hopes had been doused in cold water.

Sahas stood up, picking up his plate in his hands to put it in the sink. "You don't need to do that," Dayanand's sudden loud voice made him spin around. "We have maids to do that. It's not your job. Leave the plate there and go to college." He was signalling the nearby servant with the finger to come and pick up the plate.

"I'm fine this way," Sahas gazed at him evenly, perhaps taking a look up close for the first time. "I may not be well versed with forks, knives and napkins, but my mother taught me some manners. Though she's not around, her principles never die. Besides, both my hands are in good condition," he grunted. Back then, there had never been a single day when he had left his plate for someone to pick up and wash. Dayanand might do it with the riches he'd earned, but not him.

Saying so, he stormed into the kitchen, washed his own plate taking satisfaction in doing so, put it on the rack and walked off past Dayanand.

But what irritated Sahas was that Dayanand hadn't put out even a bit with his harsh tone.

It was dark, so intensely silent it felt as if he had been sleeping deep inside a web of darkness, catching up on lost slumber. Suddenly, a muffled noise from somewhere around woke him, making him sit up in bed. In the still of the night, Avinash darted his eyes across the room, searching for the source of that noise. But he couldn't see anything. It must have been the breeze that had rattled the window he told himself and went back to sleep. When he was just about to squeeze his eyes shut, something caught his eye, off to the right. There was something flickering on and off in the distance, like a light. Avinash got down and walked towards it. Rubbing his gooey eyes, he knelt down and brought his face up close to it. It wasn't the light. It looked more like a fogged image. To his surprise, the image slid a puff of fog, like hands to his hands and then led him somewhere. Gripping it with a blind trust, he followed it silently. They stood on his tiny balcony side by side for a long time in still silence. The gentle breeze among trees, the chirping of night birds, everything around went mute.

From the corner of his vision, Avinash could see the image staring up at the sky. He tipped his gaze up in the same direction where a million stars were gleaming, but he could only witness the darkness. He wondered where all the stars were hiding. When he looked back at the subtle image, he sensed something deep inside him drawing him to which he wanted to give in, get seized by for the image looked familiar, intimate, like he had known it so well and touched it from very near.

His heart tugged to call out the name.

"Aarti," he said slowly through numb limps.

But the image kept staring at the sky.

"Aarti, please, look at me once," he said through a lump that had lodged in his throat.

The image slowly lowered, turning up to Avinash. Tears welled up in his eyes. He knew it was her all the time. He couldn't be wrong. He wanted to ask her many things.

But then suddenly, his heart burned like it roasted in fires, his lower body felt ripped off its nerves. His hands went cold and his legs trembled. There was a pain. An excruciating pain in his ribs like someone had slit through it with a razor sharp knife. When he put his hands at his ribs, they went wet with blood. It looked like someone had given him a slash. The image forever shifted beside him, receding. He wanted to scream, asking her to stop, to not to go and call out for its help, but his throat was burning and the words died in his mouth. A sharp wind whipped at his eyes. The image slowly melted into a shapeless, amorphous fume like a cloud as he watched it blinking, and then escaped into one of the brightening stars. Avinash could now clearly hear the voices around him – the breeze, night birds chirping. He could see the million stars as well. But his eyes drifted to shut down as he could no longer stand the pain. He collapsed on the floor with a thud, gasping for air. Gradually he felt the breath slowly escape from him. And then he receded in to earlier darkness.

Avinash woke up in his bed startled, breathing heavily. His hair was dishevelled, face beaded in sweat. His hands were wet, as if they had been dipped in cold blood. His heart was still burning, just the way it had in his dream. But it was a bright morning, light spilling through open curtains.

What was it, a dream? He wondered aloud. But it had felt so real, so vivid. In fact, it was more like a nightmare. And what was it trying to convey? What were that blood and knife, and the foggy image all about?

"Aarti," he said slowly, unaware he was talking, and unaware he was weeping.

Sahas walked out of the college campus in the evening, his head hung low, footsteps taking snail pace and headed towards the nearby bus stop. Just as he reached, he spotted a black, shiny car that was parked a few meters away from the bus stop heading towards him and pulled up by his side. The driver rolled down the window and got down, engine left running. It was Dayanand's driver.

"Sir has sent the car to fetch you home safely." He said, held opening the door for him.

Sahas felt a surge of irritation. Had Dayanand appointed a chauffeur/stalker to keep an eye on him about his whereabouts? Coz, from the day he'd left the house at night and didn't show up until next morning, this driver had been literally stalking him. He felt furious with Dayanand. How could he even think that he could establish a claim on him? His ruthless persona and wealth might have the maids wash his bum perhaps, but for Sahas it'd be far more satisfying in doing things on his own. Just because he was living in the same house, things wouldn't change.

"Or, would you prefer to drive?" the man offered politely. Sahas had learnt driving back in his village when tourists had poured into his hotel. He used to drive them around showing them the history of the village. "Look Mister, I have no interest on either being driven or driving this buffalo," Sahas wanted to say, but the words died on his lips. It was the familiar figure standing on the side walk, arms folded across his chest, eyes rummaging curiously in all directions that made him swallow the urge to chide.

It was Avinash. Even from far, Sahas could sense his body shrunken, weak, the sinful charisma nowhere on the face. How long had it been they even saw each other? A month or two or maybe more, Sahas had no track. The taste of wrath momentarily weakened looking at his friend's rush of joy at the sight of him. But the next moment, the betrayal washed over him like a huge tide and he made a sudden decision.

"Okay, let's go," Sahas said, swinging inside the passenger seat and shut the door. The driver made his way around the front of the car and climbed inside the driver seat. As the engine shifted into gear, Sahas rolled down the tinted window, resting his elbows, only to see Avinash freeze his walk down the sidewalk, a defeated look on his face.

Soon, the car rattled down the crowded road, past the disappointed Avinash and joined other vehicles and pedestrians.

Avinash stood in a cloud of dust, like something precious had been stolen from him. His love had been stolen by death, his drawing skills had been stolen by his own emptiness and now his friendship had been stolen by bitter anger. He was so lonely. He felt he'd collapse under the weight of the loneliness.

Leaning against the balustrade in the balcony under the star-filled sky, Sahas gazed down at the garden. But what he saw wasn't the glowing lanterns amid plants which would be a guaranteed soothing sight more in the nights than in the mornings. But he saw his own reflection of loneliness and wrath. It had been growing like a mammoth tree, eating him from inside in the process of making its own space. He hadn't had a clue it was the seed he planted deep inside his mind, 'avenge,' the destructor of self-joy. From the moment he encountered Avinash, Sahas couldn't put out the anger swelling with every passing minute. He had no clue that one's anger could have the mysterious power to multiply the loneliness. He felt so restless and annoyed, and for a moment, his heart craved for a company to unburden his vent up frustration. Just then, he heard a knock on his door that was left half-open.

Sahas looked back over his shoulder.

It was Dayananad. He was casually dressed in night pyjamas, looking relaxed, suggesting that he was about to hit the bed. It was half-past nine and Dayanand always strictly followed his regime, save for the occasional late evening meetings which he had ended anyway.

"Can I come in?" he asked.

Sahas didn't respond. Of course he could, after all it was his house.

Dayanand took his son's silence as an affirmative and came inside, because he knew if he didn't, he would end up outside the door all day.

"You didn't have your dinner. I waited for you," he said, standing beside his son on the balcony.

Sahas said nothing.

"It's very late. You shouldn't go to bed on an empty stomach," he said and moved little closer, watching Sahas who looked as lost as always. "You've been here for nearly three weeks and yet you still behave like a stranger," Sahas shot him a snappy look. "Of course, I understand that you've been recovering from a massive tragedy and have been forced to live with me without your consent. But how long will you stay this way? You've to realize you're punishing yourself for nothing."

Sahas wondered aloud, that if this man could analyze him like a well-trained psychiatrist, then why didn't he understand that he wanted to be left alone?

"Please Sahas, come and have something." Dayanand added in a concerned voice.

"Don't start in on me now. I'm already pissed off enough for today," Sahas snapped.

But Dayanand stood there in an uncompromising stance, displaying patience at his son's sullen mood for a long while.

"You wouldn't give up, would you?" Sahas finally said, not looking at him.

Dayanand shook his head. "If you said I'd have to stand here all night to make you eat something, I would."

For some reason, Sahas grinned wickedly followed by a dense silence. He then asked. "Can I get a drink?"

Dayanand looked at him startled. Was he dreaming or something? He became unusually excited. "Of course, of course, why not," he faltered with his words. "What are you fancying for, Rum, gin, vodka, whisky? Pick your choice, just name it," he was speaking hastily, anxiety making him so. For the first time he was proud of his well-stocked bar where one could spend hours, burying one's troubles.

"As you like," Sahas shrugged. It was still a mystery to even himself he had said so.

Before his son changed his mind, Dayanand quickly went downstairs before saying, "But you must have something along with it. You can't go on empty stomach."

It wasn't long after he was back with a mature Irish whisky, two shot-glasses, a bucket of ice and some snacks. In excitement, he even forgot there were maids to do that job or it was that he wanted to derive every bit of pleasure of serving his son. He went to a corner table, hastily arranging everything. His eyes dripped with gratefulness as though his day was made with this simple act of his son's tolerance. How could he explain it couldn't match the joy of signing a crore deal agreement either?

Sahas watched him in silence, not able to help the wonder how fit and strong Dayanand looked? He knew people often mistook him for being in his late thirties. Perhaps playing with money could fetch you anything.

"You know, my son, this is a fantastic fifteen-year old Irish whiskey. One of my clients gifted it to me on my business trip to Dublin. It's such a pleasure just to sip it," he said filling up the glasses with ice. He then expertly poured two-fingers of whiskey, added a splash of water and stirred.

Sahas had never heard this man calling anyone a friend; he either called people clients or customers. Besides, Sahas had never heard of such exotic drinks before. The only drink he knew was the cheap beer Avinash used to buy from the local liquor shop on weekends. They would sit on their tiny balcony under the open sky and sip their beers slowly, munching roasted peanuts and chatting away. Damn those thoughts and damn those memories, Sahas thought furiously. He needed company, to blank out everything. For today, he didn't bother if it had to be bloody Dayanand.

"Come, my son," Dayanand gestured towards the table on which was arranged the whisky and a bewildering array of food stuffs one would find exhausting to choose from.

Sahas's eyes jumped from the table to Dayanand and back to the floor.

A moment later, all the drinks and stuff were transferred to the floor with Sahas and Dayanand sitting side by side, two feet apart with a mixture of embarrassment and uneasiness between them.

They sipped their drinks in silence for a long moment until Dayanand broke the silence. "You know, my son, I felt so happy this morning when you picked up your plate and washed it saying that your mom had taught you that. She was such a sweet lady," he said warmly, eyes shining with her memory. Perhaps the alcohol was making him blurt out his inner feelings. "Believe it or not, but I love her so much."

Sahas resisted the urge of tossing his drink at his face and yelling not to call him son again. "Then why did you leave her?" he asked. He hadn't meant to, but it just shot out of his mouth, perhaps the dizzy spell of alcohol started its magic on him too.

Dayanand lit the cigarette, smoking without hurry with a bewitching grace, eyes staring off into the distance. "My Dad," he then said slowly. "He was a business baron, a great visionary and was very influential. He gave me everything I've ever wanted. I was a juvenile then with no clarity of future and was just playing with his money until better came along. That was the same time when I met your mother. Needless to say, I fell in love with her at the first sight," he paused taking a long drag until the smoke rose up in spirals. "And then he suddenly fell ill. He was bed-ridden for a long time. It was then that the responsibility of his business empire fell on my shoulders, on a person who never knew what working hard was. I had tried to tell him many times about your mom, but I lacked the courage with his given condition."

"Was that your only excuse?"

"No," he shook his head. "When my father passed away eventually, the burden fell on me. Not only did I start the business from scratch, but I worked doubly hard to keep the empire from falling apart. People muttered behind my back that I was stupid, but I kept moving, pushing beyond my capacity, building every block, making it successful. I wanted it to be a tribute to my father." He sighed. "But by then, I was locked in a cage of responsibilities from which I couldn't escape. I had no time for myself," he said truthfully.

"So a business and a family cannot run together?" Sahas said, taking a sip of his drink. If that was the case, then no man or woman can ever run a family.

"No, I wouldn't say that. But I'd say they are two different coins and when you're forced to pick one…"

"You picked 'career'," Sahas finished, glaring at him. "Coz, you weren't able to pull back yourself from the comfort and luxury." He couldn't keep the sarcasm away from his voice. How could he explain family dynamics to such a person who was better versed with securing clients than forging relationships?

Dayanand looked back at his son, his gaze un-wavered, much to his irritation, he was smiling. "You think businesses people are ruthless, that we may be, perhaps to the demanding situations that stand in our path daily, forcing us to thrive. But try living one day like us and you'll realize what we go through. Besides, I never wanted to be in a rat race, but now that I've started, I wanted to be the fastest rat. You could neither come out nor stay inside the race now," he said, miserable pain beneath his strong face.

Not a word of what he had said had registered in Sahas' mind. He had never understood complicated things in his life. "Then again, believe it or not, but I love your mother so much and so do you," Dayanand's voice suddenly turned as soft as melting butter. There was a brief pause before he went on. "I don't have track of how many times I went back to her, pleading, begging, and asking her to accept me. But she wouldn't listen. She regarded me as a disloyal, coward person and denied me firmly. With every passing day, the hopes of her ever getting back were diminished. And then it tired me out. I gave up and had to let it be. I suddenly formed an unusual fondness for solitude. Years passed. When I learned she bore you, I went back to her hoping she'd let me take you in my arms," he shook his head, his eyes stirring up with memories, the cigar making back and forth from his lips. "But she won't allow me. So I always ducked behind a massive tree and stole glances at you. You sitting on a rock watching the waterfalls, playing around only with one guy about your age I suppose, or helping your mom in the hotel with your little hands. I observed you were kind of silent. I'd fight the urge of picking your soft hands into mine and giving a bounce with my endless kisses." He smiled at his never accomplished desire. "But I'd stand there watching you until the sky turned dark and then would go back to my big, lonely house."

There was heavy silence for the long time. All the time Sahas listened to him, tight-lipped. For a while, a sense of anger and hatred towards Dayanand momentarily weakened. But it couldn't be measured up with the pain his mother and he had gone through. How could he make Dayanand understand that the choice of being a single parent was thrust upon her?

Dayanand lit another cigarette. "One day I had someone come to my house with news," he glanced at Sahas. "Baba. He came with the news that your mother wanted to see me. And from then I travelled back and forth, meeting her. I wish she would have forgiven me long back or I'd have never left her. But we were left with very little time." He shrugged as a matter of fact.

Sahas blinked. He no more felt disgusted. In fact, he was saddened for what was revealed to him. That the neediness, the fear of being stranded and loneliness, not to his mom but that would soon shower upon his son that had forced her to this decision, the decision of living with Dayanand. Whatsoever, there would be no forgiving, Sahas thought sombrely, not to this person whom he had hated all his life.

"Okay, forget all this," Dayanand crushed his cigarette like it was an untouchable truth and was back to his sharp voice. "What is it with you?"

"What? What is it with me?"

"I mean, why do you look like you're dying to be rescued all the time, like you've been niggling over something too much?" Sahas stared at him, their eyes locked. "Correct me if I am wrong. You can share anything with me. It might not help solve your trouble, but sure it'd unburden you."

Sahas looked away. He took a swig, the drink burning his throat, and even though he didn't want to, the words gushed out. "My life is a mess! The girl I loved is dead. My best friend cheated on me. My mother betrayed me by keeping secrets," he looked at Dayanand. "And worst of all, I am having a drink with the most hated person of my life."

That brought a wicked grin to Dayanand. He raised his glass and clinked against Sahas's glass. "That's what life is about, my son. You have no choice but to accept it."

"Can you do me a favour?"

"Of course, my son, anything for you,"

"Then stop calling me son, for god's sake. It's like spattering acid into my ears."

Dayanand nodded heavily like he was considering his request. "You know, I can never stop saying that," he paused briefly, "my son." he enunciated the last word and burst out into laughter until tears sprang up into his eyes. "Okay, okay, leave all that," he wiped the tears with his hand looking at the dirty look Sahas gave. "Tell me about the dead girl and cheating business?" he said, shoving a handful of chips into his mouth, making a loud crunching sound as though he was gearing up to listen to a movie story.

"Come on, go on, my son," he insisted again.

Sahas stirred the drink debating if he should open up or not. His instincts said he shouldn't, but when did he listen to his instincts? So he went on.

By the time he had recited the entire story, the old Irish whisky bottle had been replaced with Trollinger followed by vodka. Dayanand listened to every word with rapt attention, tight-lipped, eyes staring off into the distance, perhaps visualizing everything, despite his own judgment. He then excused himself to fetch another drink. "No, I think I'll sleep now," Sahas said in a sluggish manner.

"Are you sure?"

"Yes, I am."

"Okay," Dayanand nodded taking few swaying steps until the door. He suddenly froze and spun around. "You know what they say, my son?" His voice dropped to a low, urgent murmur. "When you don't punish the evil, then you'll be the slave of that sin forever. Just remember that." For a moment it felt as though he was trying to target at someone or something, then the moment was gone. "Good night son." He shut the door.

Sahas sat on the floor, his legs stretched, staring up at the ceiling for a long while. His body felt so light – like an air-filled balloon flying on clouds with the effect of drink in his every vein – though his mind was still alert. Dayanand's prodding about his love had brought him memories of his friend's betrayal. Avinash had changed the very definition of a friend. How could someone do that? A fresh wave of infidelity hit Sahas. He burned with rage, unable to control the anger that had been buried for he knew it had to burst one day. Before he knew, he stormed out of the room fuming, not realizing anger could bring out one's evil side and do irreparable damage to relationships. He marched downstairs and looked around for the car keys. Spotting them on the key holder hanging on the wall, he grabbed them and exploded out of the house. The car that he had denied to get into that morning stood in the garage behind the house, all shiny, as though waiting to be driven by him. Without exercising any forethought, he got inside the car, cranked up the engine and drove away in the dark. Dayanand never took notice at his son.

●

Lonely and lethargic, Avinash tried to found solace in what he did best – drawing! Wasn't this his escape to drown the miseries? He set up an easel in the middle of the room and used all his concentration to draw images on the white paper before him, even though it seemed impossible. His hands shook like never before, his face turned haggard with heavy lines of weariness unlike his usual vibrant face. There was sadness about him that spoke volumes, the one a person carries in an attempt to suppress the pain they were going through. He started to take random leaves from the college and refrained from going out. He went to bed early, as if he was exhausted, even though he hadn't done anything and then slept like the dead. Sometimes, he woke up in the middle of the night, covered with sweat, trembling like he had had a nightmare or he'd have dreaded visions in the dark making him stiffen in the bed.

Now, standing in front of an easel, his hands looping in circles over the sheet, his eyes snapped to the door to the abrupt noise. It was Sahas who had shoved open the door and had marched inside. He looked like a ferocious tide under the pull of full moon that was ready to swallow you in one swig. Avinash neither flinched nor was taken aback as though he was anticipating this sudden visit.

"I knew you'd come one day. How are you Sahas?" he said, his eyes still on the easel, hands never stopping. For a moment he sounded stupid for that was all he could manage to say. Sahas didn't respond. He'd come here to settle scores, not to have a friendly chat over a cup of coffee on their terrace. All his pent-up frustration had to come out and today was the day. He sank on the bed silently and stared at the floor. An eerie silence filled the room, the same room that had once been vibrant and vivacious with the laughter and chatter of two best friends. Destiny had clearly hurled a bolt into their lives and pure friendship making them upside down.

"Why did you do that to me?" he finally asked, the question that had been distressing him for months.

There was a momentary pause on Avinash's hands. He was indeed glad Sahas had asked him about it finally. Avinash put the pencil down and walked over the window. Standing with folded arms he gazed at the crumpled papers lying on the floor, the sign of his frustration. There was a lot to answer to his friend's single question. But where should he start from?

"What did I do to you?" he then asked.

Sahas glanced at him, face flushing with anger. "You better drop it Avinash, this innocent, fake face. It doesn't suit you." He spat with sarcasm. "How could you do it to me, how could you cheat on me, your best friend? You knew how much I loved Aarti. It was you! You were the first one to know about my love. I hadn't even told mom about her. Couldn't you see how broken and shattered I was? How did you have the heart to do such a thing?" he spoke quickly and loudly, now that all the words he'd rehearsed for endless nights had been coming out.

Avinash was still staring at the crumpled, ripped papers on the floor realizing that was what he was exactly feeling right now."I didn't do anything, Sahas," he said with an honest determination.

If only Sahas could see his friend's unflinching loyalty. He shook his head obstinately. "You thought I was a fool, an idiot. By thinking so, you made a fool of yourself. It was my mistake, after all, believing you to be my friend. I should have known you better. There should have been someone to caution me that you are like a sweet poison. Sweet on the surface and a nasty monster from inside," he said with such distaste that for the first time it shook Avinash's posture as he uncomfortably shifted on his foot, his heart clenched. "You don't know how broken I am from inside," Sahas went on, his voice suddenly taking a soft side. "I feel disgusted whenever I see an artist and your face flashes the next moment. Years of trust and friendship, you broke them just like that. I hate myself for still wanting your friendship somewhere deep inside. The longing is disgusting." he said, tears brimming up in his eyes.

Avinash's heart moved momentarily at the fact that his friend, deep inside, still wanted his friendship. He stifled the urge to comfort him with an embrace, but not before giving a piece of his mind.

"You know nothing Sahas," he shook his head, "The raw truth, the pain and the agony. And here you are standing in front of me and giving definitions about them. You were always like this, right from your childhood. You believe what you see; worse, you see things through the tinted glasses of negativity, the only way you wanted." He said, suddenly thinking about the times they had spent together and how he had sacrificed his love for him. He had done so much for his friend and in the heat of the argument he asked himself, if their places were ever reversed, what Sahas would do. Would he ready to sacrifice his love for him? Or think that it wasn't really worth throwing your love away for a guy?

"What raw truth are you talking about?" Sahas walked up to him, face flushed with fury. "The drawing, that bloody drawing you drew. The one in which you and Aarti..." he glared at Avinash, fists clenched at his sides. "The one I tore to pieces when I chanced upon it? And the one I burnt, crouching at the fire, my heart burning just like it?"

Avinash was stunned to silence. "You burnt the drawing?" his voice was a whisper. How could he? How could he burn the last memory of Aarti? In the moment of rage, he wanted to thrust his fists into his friend's ribs. Sahas no more looked like a friend. He looked like a strange animal.

"Yes, I burned the drawing." Sahas took satisfaction in saying so. "The truth is that you had feelings, sexual feelings for the girl I loved. You manoeuvred behind me to win her favours." He said the word 'sexual' through gritted teeth.

That was it. Something inside Avinash snapped, perhaps the patience he had been holding for a while. He took a deep breath, steeling himself and marched towards the easel. He took the pencil back and started drawing furiously, forcing his trembling hands to be still, perhaps refraining from the urge to hit Sahas. How could his friend even imagine something like that? They say trust is the backbone of any relationship to survive and the very thing had been missing in his friend.

Sahas watched him repugnantly, confused.

Time stretched to a minute or two or three. It was silent except to the sound of breeze whistling through the opened window accompanied with Avinash's strokes.

"Wasn't it the reason you drew her naked, come on, tell me?" Sahas looked into his eye, challengingly, unable to stand the silence. It's like he wanted to get him to fight.

Avinash glared back, making a point not to blink. "Yes, I had feelings for Aarti. And you know what, she came into my life before you even met her and loved her." He finally said, no more dreading the conversation. That's enough about this business. Today had to be a day for an end to all misunderstandings.

Sahas blinked, for a moment tongue-tied.

"The truth wasn't the one you cooked up all by yourself. It was something else."

Feeling nauseated, his heart thumping heavily, Sahas said, "And the drawing…"

Avinash cut him off, holding his gaze. "And that licensed you to view things as per your perception? Take it the way you want Sahas, but I loved Aarti with all my heart and so did she. We shared intimate thoughts, intimate secrets, and intimate moments together and yes, we shared a bed too. But neither did I intent to explain nor make you understand that it hadn't been just sex between us, not just the random coupling of two bodies? And that it had been an intimate closeness that expressed how deeply we loved each other without ever breathing a word."

Sahas froze in his place, petrified, like he had swallowed a knife. He wanted him to stop, not say any other word, but it was too late.

"And that was the moment I depicted our love hoping it'd a gift to her, but…" a cloud passed through Avinash's eye as he stared out the window, pencil loosened in his hands. "You don't know how much it hurts when the person you love most hates you the most. I can still see her eyes screaming for my love and adoration. Aarti was my girl, my love, who gave a huge chunk of her life to sleep with me, trusted me and loved me madly."

Tears rolled down his cheeks as he forced the words around a lump, "And I on the other hand, stood like the dead, burying my unfathomable love for her all in the name of sacrifice, for a friend who doesn't even have the slightest faith in me. She perhaps wanted to teach me a lesson, a lesson I could never forget for the next ten births. So she left me the ache that I will have to endure my whole life."

Sahas stared at Avinash crumpled. But that didn't stop Avinash from going on. Sooner or later, the truth had to be told.

"I should have told you all this before, but I kept mum for your sake and for your friendship's sake after I learned about your love, though I'd been shattered. But you burnt the only memory I was left with, my last memory." He gave a sharp, cutting look that meant to inflict shame in him.

Sahas's gaze faltered. He was too dumbfounded to say anything. There were tears in his eyes too. But Avinash had no clue whether they were the result of guilt or the fact Aarti loved Avinash. He had lost his ability to read anyone's mind since the time his friend had labelled him a traitor.

"Aarti is mine, no matter if she's alive or dead. She's always mine. It was you who came into our lives and shattered them into pieces!" Avinash roared, his finger pointing accusingly at his friend. The pain he was going through had overshadowed every other emotion.

The friends who stood on either side of the easel looked like sworn enemies for a girl in a star, though they knew she only lived in their collective memory like a treasure that could never be found. Perhaps, Aarti might be staring down from one of those brightly lit stars in the sky, gathering her fellow stars to show them how much power a girl's love can have.

A dense silence followed between them.

A moment later, Sahas spun around, his face dropped, defeated, all the sap drawn out. He could barely stand. His legs trembled as he stumbled towards the door and left without a word.

But Avinash didn't run after him. He watched him go, perhaps one of the hardest things he had ever done in his life. But he had to! He was fed up running in the hamster wheel of misunderstandings, pleadings, denying. Now that the truth had been told, relief washed over him. Sahas had every right to know the truth, no matter how hard it'd be to digest. And above all, he had to come back to Avinash on his own accord.

But why was it that Avinash was feeling like a significant vein had been ripped out of his heart?

Sahas walked out of the room in a daze, wordless after hearing what his friend had to say. It took strenuous effort to open the car door and slide into the driver seat. Not knowing where to go, he inserted the key into the ignition, unbuckled. He hadn't realized his hands were trembling until they were set on the steering wheel. He felt too drained and naked to endure the new revelations made by his friend. And tears were a very long way to express the shock and blow he felt. As he drove, he paid no attention to where he was going, everything in front of him blurring. What was he feeling right now? Guilt, for mistaking his friend to be a culprit; or shock at this unexpected news; or misery for bringing so much grief to others; or jealousy for his best friend had a genuine affair with the girl he loved. How thoughtless of him to even think Aarti loved him. Conflicting emotions swirled in his head. Only, he, the real Sahas knew what he was up to. 'Aarti is mine, no matter alive or dead.' Sahas had not realized the car was whizzing at an uncontrollable speed, his ears echoing his friend's words. So, everything was real, the drawing he had come upon which he thought was a fantasy piece and condemned it as an act of betrayal and deceit without reflecting upon it. The very thought shook him from head to toe, making him look hopelessly hounded.

'It was you who came into our lives and shattered them into pieces.' Sahas slammed on the brakes hard, the engine roaring as his eyes failed to spot the big pothole until it came right in front. The car took a quick jounce as it slid over it, tyres squealing with gravel shooting from its sides, refusing to stop. And then it bumped into an enormous tree with a loud thud. Everything happened in a flash.

Just as it happened, the car gave a long blaring noise and Sahas's head smashed hard against the steering wheel. Everything descended into darkness.

Sahas struggled to open his eyes, but he couldn't. The pain was unendurable. Not just his eyes, but his head was throbbing too and so was his right hand. It was like he was carrying the weight of dozens of donkeys, especially on the right side of his body. When he slowly brought his left hand up to his head, there was a golf ball sized bruise on his forehead. Bandages were wrapped around his head and ankle and an IV drip was linked to one of the hands. The room was thick with heavy, pungent smell of antiseptic. It was silent expect the squeaking sound of gurneys accompanied with the occasional land phone ringing from a distance, which no one ever bothered to pick up.

Sahas had no track of who brought him to the hospital or when.

Lying on his back alone in the dark, his thoughts miles away, he stared up at the ceiling from where a long, rickety, three-wing fan was rotating slowly until a uniformed nurse walked into the room, clutching a tray in her hands. She flipped the switch on and her face broke in to a wide grin when Sahas snapped his eyes at her. She put the tray of medicines on the bedside stool and scooted out of the room saying, "I'll go call the doctor."

Not long after, she came back with an aged doctor in the lead. There was Dayanand too, tottering few steps behind, his eyes raw and exhausted.

"I told you he'll be back to conscious shortly," the doctor said over his shoulder to Dayanand. He stood at the doorway in folded arms and shot back a tensed, grateful smile.

"How are you feeling now?" the doctor asked after a brief, routine checkup.

Sahas nodded okay.

"Are you still in pain?"

"Little," Sahas murmured.

"Obviously you'd had too much booze, so it took a day to come back to consciousness.,"

The doctor's eyes skeptically jumped from Sahas to Dayayand whose face flushed with shame like he was cursing himself to make his son drink. "Do you realize how reckless and foolish it was to do so? What if someone had been rushing at that stop or you'd hit something else other than a tree? This time you were lucky enough, but what's to say next?" the doctor went on, gently chiding Sahas.

But he neither listened nor responded. It was as though the words and people around him vanished into a bubble he had created with no sound and no light. He kept tight-lipped, his gaze glued to a painting, brow furrowed in concentration. It was hanging from the wall under a fluorescent light.

"What does that painting convey?" Sahas asked suddenly. The painting was too complicated for him to understand. It was filled with different people, diverse expressions, vivid flowers, swords and random lines in between. Sahas had never understood art. It wasn't his world, after all. It was his friend's world.

The doctor looked at him puzzled. He flicked his eyes to Dayanand and the nurse who cast equally confounded glances, thinking about the worst, as if Sahas had lost his mind in the accident. "I'm sorry. I thought I was a doctor, not an art dealer," the doctor chuckled, trying to make light of the matter. "But I'll ask someone for you," he said in an attempt to not disappoint his patient. Later, when he led Dayanand to the reception area, he said, "It's just a common symptom of anxiety from which most people will recover in a couple of days. He's absolutely fine and there isn't much to worry about. I'll be by shortly with discharge instructions."

Inside the room, the nurse was left with in charge of Sahas. "Do you know how helplessly drunk you were when you were brought to the hospital," she said in a high, ringing voice, slowly undressing the bandages to apply ointment. She went on to explain how his dad had rushed him here in sheer panic when someone had notified him about his son's accident after finding his visiting card inside the car. "At first, he was very upset, having to admit you into this small hospital," she grumbled. "But there were no other hospitals nearby so he had no option. How can someone judge a hospital's services by its interiors?" She rolled her eyes in hurt pride that someone had criticized her hospital and then smiled. "Maybe every father feels the same way. They panic and get scared just like your dad. In fact, he has been constantly checking on you, like every hour, whether you were awake or not, whether you are fine or not. Oh god, sometimes he got on my nerves," she shook her head exhaustingly.

Sahas turned his head the other way, half listening, his mind filled with endurable thoughts.

"Am I speaking too much? God, old habits never die." She gathered all the things and put them back into a box. When she was about to exit, she heard Sahas from behind.

"When am I going to get discharged?"

"Right off." The nurse said before shutting the door.

After he had been discharged from the hospital, Sahas spent most of his days in his room at Dayanand's house. A miserable week slid by with Sahas in bed, unable to carry on his normal activities. It was Dayanand who helped him brush his teeth, change his clothes and have a shower daily, though they both kept mum throughout the routines. Although the servants in the house insisted that they'd take care of Sahas, Dayanand refused to let them and did everything himself. Maybe he was trying to recoup the lost time with his son and was trying hard to express that his son meant more to him than business or anything in the world.

But Sahas always looked diminished, something essential stripped away from him. There was a weight of unspoken tragedy hanging over him. Every day he woke up with a huge void inside him, feeling brittle and weak as deadwood, ready to collapse at any time. He had all his meals inside his room, held zero communication with the outside world and never left the room. It was a common sight of him in the balcony on a long chair, his chin resting on the elbows, staring off into nothing for hours and hours, his thoughts millions of miles away. When there was nobody at home, he'd stroll around, his shoulders drooped and would weep without a change in his expression. A silent weep, tears swelling and trickling down until he went back to his room and slept.

But in those quiet moments, silent walks and weeps, his mind would circle over his mother, Aarti and then finally Avinash, the three essential people in his life who no more shared anything with him. Sometimes, he wished someone would come and rescue him by rooting out all the unwanted thoughts that were sprouting like weeds inside his head. But no matter how much he tried to keep them at bay, they kept crawling back, for the weed had turned into a massive tree.

One sunny morning, Sahas dragged himself out of bed with a firm determination not to confine himself to his room as he had been doing for a week. As a start, he decided to have his breakfast in the dining hall, and not behind the closed doors of his room. And then perhaps, he'd take a stroll around the garden that was welcoming everyone with its newly-bloomed lilies. When he came downstairs, he spotted Dayanand in his customary suit around the table, all set to leave for office.

Dayanand looked over the paper he was reading, relief washing over him at the sight of Sahas. "Good to see you here, my son."

Sahas silently made his way around the table. "I am sorry, I am almost done. I'm just about to leave for office. You can go ahead." Dayananad said quickly, putting the paper down, assuming his presence would leave his son inconvenient who rather preferred solitude.

Sahas leisurely pulled a chair, sat on it and then said almost in a whisper, "It's all right. We can have breakfast together." Sheer happiness filled Dayanand's face.

Sahas was served breakfast, which he started to nibble in still silence.

"How are you holding up now?" Dayananad asked tending himself a cup of coffee.

Sahas shrugged, staring down at his plate, his hands making random circles on the food. His gesture suggested boredom and restlessness.

"Are you bored?"

Sahas shook his head, although he was helplessly bored and drained.

Dayanand leant back in his chair, sipping his coffee amid awkward silence. The only time they spoke at length was the night they had got tipsy together.

"You look better now, but I had been worried about you," he finally said, breaking the silence.

"You need not. I know how to take care of myself." The words sounded shallow to even himself as Sahas said. He recalled how Dayanand had come to him tiptoed every night, pulled a chair and sat, staring at Sahas, stroking his head gently, unaware that his son was pretending to sleep.

Dayanand nodded before blowing into the cup. "If there's something, I can resolve…" he watched him over the rim of the cup.

Sahas shook his head. "I had my own reasons," he said, his jaw firmly set.

"It's good when you learn to rely on yourself."

Just then a servant emerged from the kitchen and put some pills on the table. He reminded Dayanand that they had to be taken after his breakfast.

Dayanand grunted before swallowing them dry and winced.

Sahas couldn't help but stare at the medicines and wonder what they were taken for? Perhaps for the knee-joint pain Dayanand had been complaining with the doctor briefly the other day or the anti-depressant pills which Sahas had overheard one of the servants saying. He had no clue, but he wished he could ask, feeling a tinge of shame for not attempting to, for he knew this simple act of concern would go a long way for him.

Sahas also knew that Dayananad had been clamouring for his love since the time he had stepped into this house. He had been looked after with much care, attention and boundless patience that he wished he could admire this man just the way he had his mother.

When it came to his own behaviour, Sahas couldn't help but mull over the way he'd been living disconnected with the outside world, leastwise bothering about others' feelings. Hadn't he always blamed the people around him for his plight? Take for instance his mother or friend or Dayanand. What had he contributed to the few close relationships in his life? Nothing possibly. At least his Dad was trying to fix the crumpling relation with him. It was then that Sahas realized with a pang that this was the first ever time he had considered Dayananad as his dad, at least in his thoughts. But what he hadn't yet realized was that he was already on the way to forgiving him.

"Well, I have a meeting to attend in just about an hour," Dayanand rose to his feet, bringing Sahas back to senses. "If you're feeling too bored, go for a ride around," he donned his coat and then paused. "I mean take the driver," he added as a presumptive caution.

Just as he was about to leave, Sahas startled him with his request. "Can I come to your office with you?"

Sahas looked at his reflection in the mirror. A pale face with hollow eyes, sunken temples, thick beard which he had neither shaved nor trimmed for months, stared back at him. To sum up, he looked like an old Santa Claus without any gifts to share. It wasn't that he hadn't had the time to fix his body. He had been so neck deep in the gloom of his upside down world that he had lost all interest in his own body. Now, as the realization dawned upon him, he wanted to put some effort into his appearance as he was visiting his dad's office. It took him nearly an hour to transform to his normal self. When he came downstairs all trim and smart, Dayananad looked at him with startled admiration.

"You look like a potential client ready to pitch a business deal," he smiled throwing his hands up in the air.

Sahas smiled back without any hint of a smirk. He really liked his dad's remark of 'potential client', Once the same remark would have upset and agitated him, when would this idiot realize that a son had to be complimented as 'smart' or 'handsome' or 'gentleman' and not as an asshole client?

"It's because of the outfit you bought me," his eyes twinkled as he looked down at the classic blue spread collar shirt paired with cream-coloured trousers that his dad had chosen for him. Sahas couldn't hold back a tinge of gratefulness in his voice. But only people who were intimately connected to him would have sensed it. For instance, his friend Avinash who was an expert at reading faces. If he were here, he would have playfully punched Sahas on his shoulder, pulling his leg saying that he had started liking his dad. Also, he'd have advised him to leave all the hatred behind and start a new relationship. But Dayanand, who was under a firm presumption that no matter what efforts he put in, his son would always consider him as a selfish wolf, hadn't been able to perceive the gratitude in his son's voice. Sahas sat in the front passenger seat, staring out the window, as the car veered to the expressway. Unlike every day, Dayanand drove the car refusing the driver's offer. A slow melodious music was playing on the car's music system, sparing Sahas the jitters he had been feeling inside. It was still a mystery as to why he was visiting his dad's office in the first place. Maybe he wanted to get out for a breath of fresh air. If so, he could go for a stroll or visit his college which he'd stopped going for a while, or do endless other things. But no, he chose to be a companion to his Dad, or wanted his Dad's companion to overcome the loneliness. It was funny how relations take a sudden, sharp turn in one's life. People whom one considered enemies may turn into well wishers and vice-versa. Maybe it was all to do with one's perception. And for Sahas, nothing had changed expect his thinking. So far he had looked at his dad with a closed heart and everything seemed wrong and selfish. Now he had started to look at things with an open heart and positive vibes were engulfing him. As the car pulled up at Rota India, Sahas lingered in his seat for a moment. He couldn't quite get over the fact that this was the same office he had jostled inside months earlier and broke down at Dayanand to all jaw-dropping faces of the employees.

Now, walking behind the blissful Dayanand, his head lowered, Sahas felt sick with nerves. To his embarrassment, Dayanand paused at every passerby, cubicle, introducing his son. For one mad moment, Sahas considered to crawl under the table or run away without a backward glance. When Dayanand sensed the same on his son's face, he murmured reassuringly, "Don't worry my son. It's quiet natural to freak out. I am doing this for your own good. Just lift your chin up or blindly follow me."

Sahas did just the way he'd suggested; to his surprise, the shyness slowly diminished.

A moment later, Dayanand took Sahas for a tour around his chic modern office. He was then led to Dayanand's personal cabin where everything from the chairs to the floors and false ceiling was painted in a fresh cream colour, giving it a classy look. Dayanand phoned his personal secretary asking him to drop by with the bunch of latest files. Not long after, the man walked in with files in his hands, weight-of-the-world expression. It came as a surprise to him when Dayanand asked him to explain the latest projects and ventures to his son. He even dropped hints that few dealings from hereunder would be handled by his son. Dayanand was speaking quickly, with full vigour, contrary to his grave, serious manner. Suddenly, he had a vision of his son walking beside him in a classy suit, discussing the business around their office. As delicious and relieving as the idea seemed, he deep down knew the truth that his son could never be related to running a company.

The secretary gasped at the very suggestion. It sounded so immature and foolish. For a person to handle such dealings, years of training were necessary. And everyone knew that Sahas wasn't cut out for running a business. Forget about business, what did he know? How to negotiate a joint venture or break a business deal or leastwise how to dine lavishly with a customer? He hadn't a clue. And it wasn't even that these things had to be reminded to Dayanand, a person with a capacity to perceive if one can fit the business or not with a single glance. Perhaps he was blinded with the love for his son.

"I'm sorry but I don't understand a thing about your projects or work," Sahas said as though he peeked into the secretary's mind and spotted the worry. "I am here just for a change. I needed a different environment and different people to cope with my own misery. Besides, one needs vigorous training to handle such dealings. I hope you understand," his eyes flicked from the secretary and rested on Dayanand as though asking for forgiveness.

It hadn't taken much effort to read the gaze for Dayanand. He took a moment, reconsidering his opinion, which sounded too shallow once he jostled out of the dreamy world, the one where anything could happen. In fact, he himself knew well that his son was awfully incompetent and lacked the maturity or instinct to deal with business strategies. But sometimes everything can go clouded in the company of a blood relative. No matter how many years you spent apart from each other, when you come close to your loved ones, the togetherness, warmth and affection will bridge the gap in minutes. That's the power it had.

"Okay." He nodded his head silently.

Almost immediately, the secretary said. "I think he's absolutely right." He heaved a thankful sigh that he had been holding from the moment he stepped into the room. "Besides, he looks just like you sir. Now I can see what you must have looked like when you were young." He smiled.

Dayanand's face beamed at the compliment. Sahas too secretly relished that remark and it took gruelling effort to stop the flush rushing to his face. That very moment, it looked like nothing in the world could tear father and son apart.

After Dayanand left to attend a series of meetings, Sahas flipped through glossy business magazines for a long time which he found from the low coffee table. When he was helplessly bored, he ambled around the office admiring the modern-art canvas that had been dominating the reception. As he did, he caught the curious gazes, especially from the park-avenue type girls. Girls with sleek hairs in sexy outfits, craning their necks, struggling to grab a chance to make Sahas talk. Not that he looked like a Hollywood hero, but hoping to pursue a relationship with the chairman's son would be a splendid boost to their careers too. To his horror, some girls were battering their eyelashes, passing flirtatious looks. But Sahas was too shy and terrified, and lingered around the wall like he was about to diminish inside. How could he explain no matter how many beautiful girls stood in a row, it was only Aarti who came to his mind. It was she who had made him realize that he too looked handsome and was a man. For many, she might be just a dead girl living in the stars, but for him she was his only love and would be one forever.

It wore Sahas down after a long, lazy day at the office with nothing to do. He excused himself at the lunch hour to go for a stroll away from the incessant phone calls and busy people. Though Dayanand had insisted that he'd accompany, Sahas politely declined his offer and came out alone. He was aware that Dayananad stayed in the office till late, attending meetings, sifting through the uncompleted work that had piled up from weeks and didn't want to disturb him.

Just as Sahas strode along the parking lot, his hands stuffed in the pockets, whistling through the mouth, with a leap in his step, he paused for a moment at a big car. Automatically, his hands went up raking through the hair, looking at his reflection in the rearview mirror of the car. He looks just like you sir. His dad's secretary's comments echoed in his ears. He automatically straightened up, mirroring Dayanand's posture and confidence.

"Do we look similar?" Sahas wondered aloud, taking a long look at his oval face, dark brows above his honey-coloured eyes. Yes, he was undoubtedly a replica of his dad, though they were worlds apart in their natures.

For a moment, he idly wondered, how happily he could live with Dayanand if he could forgive him.

Or he already had? Yes, he had already forgiven him and that's why he had ended up here, in his office. The thought that the same blood that his dad carried in his veins, flowed in his body too made Sahas's hair stand erect. It was so senseless that it was unbelievable he started to like his Dad. Or that the truth was that he had always adored Dayananad and had wanted to meet him clandestinely, but the desolation he had caused by abandoning his mother had made him furious. Now the attention and love showered upon him had slowly made his anger fade away.

Wow, the positive vibes felt like a gentle stream in his mind. How long had it been that he felt this way? Now, he wouldn't want to keep these magical vibes confined to him. He'd share them with Dayanand too, no with his dad. And tomorrow would be a perfect day, Sahas decided. It was his birthday, after all, a special day. Before Dayanand surprised him with his first gift, he'd surprise him with this news.

When he was clouded over with the newly-bloomed relationship, something caught his attention. It was the guy who looked very familiar, as if he was known before or seen from close quarters. Sahas eyed the guy intently for a long time trying to recall where he had seen him before. Recognition rippled across his eyes with the feeling that he had never forgotten that face.

The mysterious, red-eyed man was the same person Sahas had encountered several times before. He had seen him on his first day at college, at the small bar where he and Avinash frequently hung out, again at the hospital where he was admitted after the accident and now here, in his dad's office. Yes, he was undoubtedly the same guy! We tend to forget people we chance upon accidentally, but occasionally some faces leave you with a mysterious, indelible memory that one couldn't forget even in their dreams. The guy had dirty, shaggy, dry curls that looked like they hadn't been washed for years above red, foxy eyes. He leant against the pillar, one of his legs bent, a half-burnt cigarette clasped between his fingers, head cocked, speaking to someone in front of him. Who was this mysterious man? And what was he doing here, in his dad's office parking lot? Sahas wondered with a bubble of curiosity.

But as soon as he started to walk in his direction, the guy's posture stirred about with the realization of being watched. Noticing Sahas approaching him, the guy quickly tossed the cigarette from his hands, waved a hasty goodbye to the man in front of him and soon zipped past the vehicles.

His action came as a surprise to Sahas. The curiosity turned to alarm and suspicion when he watched the guy brisking away, every now and then snapping his head back to furtively check if he was being followed or not. Why did the guy try to run away from him? Had he known him from before? Was it deliberate, him being in the same place and at the same time as Sahas every time? Disconnected questions rattled Sahas's head as he found himself quickening his own steps, soon followed by a chase.

By the time Sahas raced down the street, the guy had plunged into the heavy traffic, darting between the vehicles aiming at a narrow, deserted lane off the street. Sahas tenaciously followed him, screaming at him to stop, ignoring the wobble in his legs and hands from healing wounds. After about a ten-minute straining chase with jumping over the walls, scraping at their toes and occasionally tripping on the road, Sahas was able to pull at the guy's legs. He fell down with a thud, his face up. Right off Sahas lunged at him, roughly grabbing at his shirt and pinned his wriggling body against the gravel.

They were both breathing hard, layered in dust with Sahas holding him resolutely, his heart pounding. He could read a sense of fear and dread in the guy's eyes that were filled with tears.

"Who are you?" Sahas asked through a dry mouth before tightening the grip around his neck.

The guy's body trembled with fear. "Please leave me. I just did whatever your dad said," he croaked.

A cold shiver ran through Sahas's spine. His hands around the guy's neck momentarily weakened as though the fear from that man had passed onto him. Sahas stooped a bit, bringing his face up close to the guy. "What did he ask you to do?" he narrowed his eyes, color draining from his face.

After his son had left, Dayanand resumed his hectic pace of work, sifting through his mails, holding management meetings and streamlining the projects. It was nearly dark when he walked out of the office. But he wasn't worn out and still had the energy to head straight to the new shopping mall that had opened on Magrath Road. Not that he was an incredible shopper, but today he was all set to blow away lot of money for it was his son's birthday the next day. Among the twenty surprise gifts shopped were a diamond Analog watch, stone leather jacket, aviator sunglasses and many more ranging from sporting equipment, music accessories, to high-tech gadgets. It was as though he frantically wanted to fill the love tank for Sahas, recouping all the lost twenty birthdays. And now that they had forged a nice bond, Dayanand wanted to bowl him over by showering gifts, hoping to define a lavish future to his son. When he reached his home with arms full of gifts, a swell of hope in his heart, Dayanand's face fell when he learnt that Sahas had already hit the bed. It was just half-past eight and he never slept so early, Dayanad worried. Perhaps it was the fatigue followed after a long day out, for it was the first time Sahas had stepped out of the house after his accident. Dropping all the gifts on the table, he changed into his night pyjamas before freshening and climbed into bed, though he never slept. Every now and then, his eyes flicked at the wall clock, waiting for the hour and minute reach 12 o'clock. He wanted to be the first one to wish his son. It was strange for he never remembered his own birthday, but the mountain of love he had for Sahas drove him insane. When it was exactly twelve, Dayanand kicked the blanket off, jumped out of his bed and scooted to his son's room excitedly. Stifling the urge to run up to his son, shake and yank him out of bed, hugging and showing him all the gifts, Dayanand stood there for a long time, before knocking at the half-open door twice. For one mad moment, he mulled over the idea of blaring the alarm in Sahas's ears like a crazy teenager, though he thought better of it. After standing for an uncountable time, Dayananad finally swivelled around, disappointment washing over his face. Maybe tomorrow morning he'd be first up to wish him.

The moment the door was shut behind him, Sahas opened his eyes wide and slid out of the bed to walk to the balcony. Under the full moon light, his eyes were evidently raw and red, anger pushing against them. All the time he'd be pretending to sleep when Dayanand stood at the door, waiting for him to stir. How on earth could sleep overtake him when his soul was crushed to pieces inside? From the moment he had learned the awful truth from that guy outside Dayanand's office, all he wanted was to go and shake Dayanand, making him tell that what he'd learned was wrong. As dreamy as the idea seemed, Sahas knew his world had already tipped upside down. Sahas stood there the whole night in the cold, his hands clasped behind him, his stomach in twists, pondering in silence, an unspoken silence that always had its own secrets.

It was an overcast morning the next day, the sun obscured by the clouds. The refreshing raindrops could touch the earth any moment. For some, the anticipation of the arrival of shower is so refreshing that they want to brace themselves up with a steaming cup of coffee in their hands. But for some, it just leaves a trail of negative feelings, just as in case of Sahas. He'd been standing stubbornly in the balcony all through the windy night, his ears repeatedly ringing with that guy's words, his soul cracked.

Dayanand had walked to his room very early in the morning eager to wish his son and shower him with gifts. But despite the repeated knocks, Sahas never opened the door that was latched from inside. Fed up of many unsuccessful attempts, Dayanand had finally left for office unwillingly, hoping to meet him later. Sahas waited until Dayanand's car whizzed around the corner street before he opened the door of his room and ran downstairs. The servants down were engrossed in their respective works as Sahas called out to everyone, including the watchman. He excitedly told them that it was his birthday and he wanted to spend the whole day with Dayananad to give him a surprise. He asked them to take the day off and warned not to return until the next morning.

They all happily nodded their heads and hugged Sahas, showering their blessings on him. When they were all about to leave the house, Sahas handed the old servant an envelope asking him to drop it in the post box. It was a letter he'd written in nostalgic tears the last night. When all the servants left, Sahas locked the front door and spun around. Standing alone in the middle of the big house amid dense silence, his heart rammed in his chest. The house looked haunted for the first time in months and he found himself hating the eerie silence.

Taking a deep breath and steeling himself, he went to the land phone that was sitting on a table in the corner of the room and dialled a familiar number.

It was Avinash's mobile number.

Sahas's heart pounded in his ears as the phone rang on the other side, for he was calling his friend for the first time since their candid conversation weeks ago. The phone rang a couple of times and went unanswered. Sahas rang again, determined to make his friend talk whatever may come.

Avinash was on his way to work on his bike when his pocket buzzed with a call. Though he ignored initially, roiled at the continuous calls, he pulled the bike to the side of road and took out the mobile from his pocket. When he glanced at the screen, it flashed an unknown land number. He reluctantly pressed the green button on his cell, brought it to his ear and the voice on other side made his heart clench. "Sahas?" he breathed.

"How are you Avi?"

The name 'Avi' sent a shiver of pleasure through Avinash's body. It was the nickname his friend used during earlier times when they were thick friends. How long had it been hearing it?

"I'm fine Sahas. How are you?"

There was a brief pause before Sahas responded. "I'm good. I wanted to talk to you regarding something very important." He could hear Avinash getting down from his bike, his entire body stiffening in attention.

"Tell me Sahas. What is it about?"

"Not on the phone, I want to meet you personally."

Avinash stared at the phone, taken aback. A gush of disconnected thoughts nerved him as he found himself wondering if his friend wanted to meet to make peace or continue to upbraid him. Whatsoever, all that mattered was the anticipation to meet him. "Tell me the place and time then."

"In our village. I want to meet you in our village."

"What?" Avinash exclaimed at the suggestion. "Where are you now?" He threw a quick glance at the number on his mobile and guessed it must be coming from Dayanand's house, though he had no clue which area it belonged to.

Sahas didn't answer him. "Avinash, do you remember the huge banyan tree near our house where we used to suspend a tire from a low branch and swing on it taking turns?" he was swirling the cord, staring off into nothing, his eyes momentarily beaming with memories, "I'm about to go to the village today to once take a tour around the places. I want you to meet me there in the evening at sharp six. What say? If you're up to it, we can meet there, could you?"

"I could try."

"Surely, you must," Sahas said urgently.

"I will." Avinash assured. "Besides, I can never forget that place till my last breath. Those days were the happiest days of my life, the days I spent with you."

A dense silence followed. Sahas's fingers tightened around the phone. Surge of emotions crushed him, his heart longing to see his friend right away. He stood on the brink of telling him everything, the awful things he'd learned, the sleepless nights he spent, everything, though he gripped his heart, saying, "Okay, I'll be waiting for you there at the mentioned time."

"Sure I would. Umm... Happy birthday."

Sahas' jaw stiffened. If he spoke for a minute more, he'd completely lose his strength to hold back the tears and along with the tears the truth would spill out. "Thanks," he said through a lump that had lodged in his throat. "No matter what, I want you to meet me in our village this evening. Please don't disappoint me." He hung up quickly, fearing Avinash would place the wobble in his voice.

Sahas shut his eyes, allowing silence to wallow him, to simmer down the screams in his mind, and then he made his way around the house, unplugged all the land phone connections to make sure that no phone was in working condition.

When he opened Dayanand's room, the sight of myriads of boxes wrapped in colourful papers lying on the bed made Sahas stand motionless for a long while. Only when he believed he could, he latched the door from inside and walked towards the gifts. Dropping down the edge of bed, he maniacally ripped opened all the gifts his dad had lovingly bought him. In every gift he opened, he could see the painstaking efforts his dad had taken to surprise him and tears streamed down his cheeks. "Why? Why did you do that?" Sahas kept mumbling under his breath repeatedly. The awful truth he learned burned like holding a poison in his throat.

Donning the new clothes, watch and all the luxury things he was gifted, Sahas went to his room and fetched his iron suitcase. Kneeling on the floor, he flipped it open before blowing specks of dust off it. It was his mother's photo his eyes fell upon that he had stuck on the inner lid of the suitcase. Plucking it, he traced his trembling fingers over it. It had been taken when she was very young by one of the tourists before Sahas was born. She stood stiff and straight like she had been ordered to, her lips in a tight smile, flashing a tensed look through her dark eyes wide open. Sahas found himself nostalgically grinning as he recalled how he'd always teased his amma, flipping the photo in his hands and said, "If you do not like a particular customer coming over to our hotel, simply give him or her this photo of yours and they would run without a backward glance."

Sahas wished she was here right now for he'd have rested his head in her lap and cried his lungs out. He thought about Aarti too, whose absence was like the smell of soaked earth after rain which you could perceive, but never actually touch or see. His gaze then shifted to the rolled drawings that sat tight in a corner of the suitcase, his most cherished belongings.

Sahas picked up each drawing, unrolled it carefully like he was handling an ancient antique. They were all his, fondly drawn by his friend Avinash. Sahas had preserved them in his suitcase and no one, not even his friend, knew that. Now, they all stared back at him, reminding him of the unfathomable love his friend had for him. Gathering all of them in his arms, Sahas glanced around the boring walls of his room. They were so flat, and had been simply painted in a dull ash colour. Expect for the lamps hooked on to the wall on either side of the bed, there weren't any interiors to gain one's attention. It was actually Sahas who had insisted that his room looked bland for he didn't want to be reminded of his dad's wealth before he came here. Now, for the next one hour, he took control of the walls as he began gluing the drawings across the wall. There were many – Sahas and Avinash sitting on a rock facing the waterfalls, on the tire swing, on the last bench of the classroom, their arms intertwined, Sahas playing with his mom, Sahas standing on a low stool and helping his mom cook, Sahas with Baba and many more. It was a treasure trove of memories and Sahas was glad he had preserved every single drawing. Once finished, he sank down on the floor, his chin resting up on elbows and watched every drawing intently on the brightened walls, a swell of pride filling his chest. He sat there wallowing in the past until his dad came back.

Sahas stood up alert, despite being lost in the harrowing thoughts of the past, when the doorbell rang. Before dashing downstairs, he looked at his reflection in the mirror, telling himself that today he was all set about to face the circumstances, no matter what destiny had in store. Heaving a deep sigh, he opened the door for Dayanand who stood in front of him looking annoyed. But soon his gaze turned to a radiant smile looking at his son all dolled up. It meant Sahas had opened every gift he'd bought.

"You look extremely handsome, my son." Dayanand took a step inside the house, his arms stretched wide for a huge hug, the impatience about there being no watchman at the gate and his constant unanswered calls waning away.

Sahas indeed looked like a rich, preppy guy just the way Dayanand had picturized when he'd painstakingly picked up every gift.

"Thanks," Sahas murmured into his neck rooted like a stone, his hands on his sides when he was enveloped in a tight hug

Dayanand pulled back, holding Sahas at an arm's length. "Happy birthday, my son. I guess I'm the last person to wish you," he grinned crookedly. "Besides, I have been trying the land phones from late afternoon, but there seems to be some problem."

Sahas jerked away from his arms, caution taking over him. "Forget about it, actually I have a small surprise for you," he said urgently.

"Surprise for me. On your birthday! You gotta be kidding me."

"No, I swear. It's all set. I was engrossed in the preparations right from the morning. Please freshen up and come to my room."

"Okay, I'll be there in ten minutes," Dayananad nodded, and called out to the servants.

"There's no one in the house," Sahas cut him off quickly. "Actually I have sent them away. I thought that only the two of us should share the special surprise." He gave a tense smile, suppressing the wobble in his voice.

Dayanand drew his eyebrows in surprise or confusion. The phones weren't working, servants were made to leave. What was his son up to? His brilliant mind could have smelled something fishy, but he was too occupied with the word 'surprise'.

To Sahas's relief, he simply nodded and went to his room. A moment later, he emerged in a pair of loose jeans and a tee-shirt looking as comfortable as ever.

The moment he entered Sahas's room, his jaw dropped open in surprise. In the middle of the room an intimate dinner had been arranged. The table had been covered with white floral linen, lemon yellow napkins arranged beautifully. A fragrant candle was burning in a candle holder beside two wine glasses and a bottle of Chardonnay.

"It looks splendid, my son. The surprise is so ama...." Dayanand's throat closed in for a moment as his gaze fell upon the drawings glued across the walls. Sahas searched for a hint of startle on his face, but he couldn't spot one. Perhaps Dayananad had expertly disguised it under his charisma. "... Simply amazing," he resumed speaking, "Thanks a lot, but don't you think it should be the other way round? You're the birthday boy, remember?"

"Yeah, I am well aware of that. Actually I want to have a candid conversation with you," Sahas said pulling out the chair for Dayanand to sit. "Mom always used to say that 'the way to a man's heart is through his stomach.' She was a great cook and taught me exceptional culinary skills. Today I thought you should taste my favourite dishes as we talk. How do you like the surprise, by the way?" He clasped his fingers, pushing a fake smile.

Dayanand smiled radiantly. "You have no idea how you had me bowled over. The lavish meals I had had couldn't stand to this meal," he extended his hands across the table. "The surprise is mind blowing. What a pleasure!" his eyes spilled gratefulness. He hadn't thought that he would be forgiven so easily. All his efforts to save the relationship were bearing fruit now.

Throughout the meal, Dayanand spoke incessantly about the new venture he had recently stumbled upon, office politics, the stiff competition their company had to weather and many more things. In between he paused to say how delicious or mouth-watering the dishes were. Sahas ate his food in silence, his eyes glued on him, listening attentively to his every word as though he'd only moments with him. For a moment, Sahas had forgotten that his world had turned upside down and it looked like they both were having a normal, chilled out meal. So beguiled was he by Dayayand's charm. After they finished the meal, Sahas took his wine glass and walked to the window overlooking the garden. Dayanand lit the cigarette and began to speak between drags. "Sahas, I know you aren't cut out for business, but I want you to groom your skills in that area. See, you can't simply go on pretending you couldn't. After all, you're the inheritor of this empire. And there's no need to panic. When my dad insisted that I should take on the business, I was terrified and apprehensive and said no. But today, look at me," he went on proudly. Sahas sipped his wine, intently gazing the drawings across the walls, never listening a word. He recalled every moment he'd shared with Avinash. What wonderful memories were they! Sahas always admired and envied the way people endeared to Avinash to his friendliness, good humour, the way he read people's mind, especially his friend's, and above all, his endowed skill of drawing.

Taking another sip, Sahas looked at Dayanand. He was still talking, smoke twirling up in impossible shapes above his head. "In fact, you're lucky to have me. I'll help you groom with all the skills needed. Let it take years Sahas, but there's no denying you should one day pick up business."

Sahas couldn't hear a thing. For him, the entire world had fallen mute. It was only the words of the man began to ring over and over in his mind. *"It's your father. It's always your father. I was just a tool used by him, please leave me. I swear I'll disappear from this city and you would never see me. Sure I'd do anything if you release me. What? You don't believe me, oh god, see for yourself poor boy."* The words were like electric shock infused waves. They rolled around his head, smashing the inside walls of the brain and pounced back giving a throbbing pain. In a sudden fit of anger, he tightened the grip on the stem of wineglass he was holding, which broke to pieces, wine spilling across the floor.

Dayanand snapped his head around. Panic stricken, he dropped the cigarette and rushed to Sahas, pulling his bloodied hand that was pierced with a shard of glass. "Oh god, you're bleeding," Dayanand cried. He fluttered around the room looking for a cloth. When he found a first aid kit, he took out cotton and dabbed at his son's hand. "What Sahas, why did you hold the glass so tight? Look at it now. You must be careful with sharp things. Is it hurting?" he asked worriedly.

"Yes, it is!" Sahas said flatly, tears stinging his eyes. How right his dad was in saying that he should be careful when dealing with sharp things, just the way one should be when dealing with sharp people. How could he make him understand that the excruciating pain that was slashing his soul was worse than the small virtual cut Dayanand was witnessing with his eyes? "Dad, how do you like the drawings?" he then asked.

Dayanand looked up startled. He wasn't still used to his son's mysterious ways of jumping from one talk to other.

"Tell me dad, how do you like the drawings?"

It was then the words registered Dayanand. A burst of emotion spilled from his eyes: It was the first time Sahas had called him dad. He was either called by his name or nothing. Hadn't he pictured it in his endless dreams, to have called 'Dad' from his son?

"You're bleeding, my son. Let me take a look at the slit."

"Why do you want to do that, Dad?"

"Do what, my son?" Dayanand didn't lift his eyes from the wound, tending it with an antiseptic solution.

"Why do you want to get Avinash killed?" Sahas said in a low whisper, his throat feeling strangled.

Dayanad's hand suddenly froze on his son's wrist. Cold shiver ran down his spine. His eyes were filled with profound fear and confusion as though he was caught unprepared.

"Tell me Dad, why you want to kill my friend?" Sahas asked in a calm, measured tone, tears welling up in his eyes. "Did you?" he hated the flicker of hope in his voice, the hope to hear that what all he'd heard was wrong. He'd experienced a range of emotions, from disbelief and shock to defeat and sorrow and now emptiness when he'd learned the awful truth. He felt stupid, not seeing beyond the polished charisma that was all glossy from outside and rotten from inside in his dad.

Dayanand fumbled for a chair to drop on as his legs wobbled. As he did, his blood ran shivering cold as though he had been immersed in freezing water, naked. A dense silence followed, the silence that was disquieting and filled with the 'whys', 'whats' and many other difficult questions a father had to answer and a son had to know.

Sahas crouched down closer to his chair. "Did you, dad?" Another unbearable silence, "Okay, dad, I wanted to tell you a little story today, a story of two young boys. Once upon a time, a young, shy boy slipped into the waters in his village. He was terrified and panic-stricken, gasping for air for he didn't know how to swim. He called for his mother, thrashing his arms, but she was probably washing her clothes along with other women.

He even called out for his dad though he knew how stupid he was to do so. The man was perhaps signing a deal behind the closed walls, unaware of the danger. And when the boy had almost lost faith in his life, drowning into the waters, suddenly his hands felt something," Sahas's eyes twinkled as he smiled at the memory, "At first he thought it was a fish, but before he recognized it was a shirt, he was pulled out from the waters and had been saved. When the boy reluctantly opened his eyes, his gaze fell upon a charming, young, vibrant face, smiling up at him. It was the moment the shy guy decided he wouldn't leave the side of his saviour, no matter what."

Sahas leaned a little forward and looked at Dayanand with a haunted look. "Do you know who the saviour was in the story?" Dayananad never looked up, his gaze faltering, "Come on dad, you're the smartest person I've ever known."

The antiseptic solution from his hands had slipped and struck the floor with a clatter.

And that was it; it was the silent answer to Sahas's question. He sank down on the floor, his hands crossed on his knees. He hadn't looked at Dayanand with disgust or detest but with a disheartening look that the rope he'd been pulled by during his despair times had now become a noose around his neck.

"But why Dad, what has Avinash ever done to you?"

Dayanand lowered his head, looking at his pale, trembling hands, "I, I... I'm sorry," his voice shook now that all the façade had been lain down.

"Sorry?" Sahas choked back a bitter laugh, appalled by his dad's apology. It was as if he had been nudged by a stranger on the road and was told sorry. "You wanted to get a person killed and you're saying sorry?"

There was a dense pause.

"Come on, you can't go on silent like this dad. You need to answer me. Do you even know whom you intended to kill?" Sahas voice raised a notch. "What had he ever done to you?"

Dayanand looked up for the first time, tears welling up in his eyes. "I'm sorry. I never intended to hurt you."

"But you already did." Sahas banged his fist into the chair. "You are a ruthless, cold-blooded man. Now I can see beyond the mask you have been wearing of a desperate dad, clamouring for love. You're more poisonous than a viper. I am ashamed to call you dad."

The anger and pain was so deep and sharp that Sahas could no longer hide his conflicted emotions. The horror of what he had learnt had petrified his feelings for his dad. But he was still clueless as to why he had taken such a cruel decision. "Please no," Dayanand shook his head, unable to bear the hatred showered upon him. This wasn't what he wanted. He wanted the love, affection he had missed all those years. "I never wanted to hurt your feelings, my son, not for anything in the world. But when I learnt about your love, I learnt that your friend had cheated on you. My blood ran cold and the demon inside me awoke. I became crazed and frustrated." He ran an anxious hand through his hair.

"Oh god, I love you a lot Sahas. I couldn't see you defeated. I just couldn't bear to see the way you were in the hospital, cheated by your best friend over a girl whom you loved a lot. My men had been following you from the time you arrived in Bangalore and when you told me about Avinash's betrayal on the day we had a drink, I went so wild. I thought it was my job to fix your damaged relationship. I didn't reflect upon the repercussions," tears trickled down his cheeks.

Sahas' eyes widened with horror. "And that made you decide that my friend had no right to live on?" He demanded in disgust, unable to stomach the heights of his dad's cruelty. "So you neatly mapped out his future, trying to eliminate him? Avinash never cheated on me, dad. My friend never cheated on me. It was I who cheated on him with my foul thoughts. He loved everyone and that was the only mistake he ever committed in his life. He loved Aarti and despite the fact that she loved him, he stepped down just for me, only for me, for his stupid friend who left him nothing but a box full of pain and hate and you wanted to get him killed?" Sahas couldn't stop recalling how he had crushed his friend with his words, with his stained feelings. God knows what he had not said to him, but despite every word he spat with hatred, Avinash kept mum, loving him back. That was the heart his friend had.

Pangs of guilt sliced his heart. "The only mistake Avinash ever did was love me madly right from his childhood. Look at those drawings Dad, the one with Mom, Baba, with him, in the school, at the waterfalls. Is there one drawing with you and me? No, there wouldn't be. Because you were never there in my life, all I had in my life was Mom and my friend Avinash. God has taken Mom away from me and now you want to take Avinash away from me? How could you even think I'd survive with that thought?"

Guilt and shame spread across Dayanand's face. "God knows what came over me, my son. It had nothing to do with bitter revenge. It was just out of the abundant love I have for you, my son. I am sorry." Dayanand's words strangely came out thick and sluggish.

To his horror, things were blurring in front of him. "How could you even think that you could shower your love on me with bloodstained hands?" Oh god, I was bogged down in a fantasy-world all this time, thinking and dreaming that our relation had been patched up and that we could live happily ever after. I was wrong. I was utterly wrong," Sahas wiped the tears with the back of his hand. "Okay, if you can think that relationships can be sustained with bloodstained hands, then let me try one."

"Please Sahas, I beg you. Please forgive me," Dayanand broke into tears. He no more looked like a strong, impregnable man that could command hundreds of people with a single wave of the hand, but like a brittle mud wall that could anytime fall apart with a slight touch.

Sahas pressed his eyes to him. "No dad, there won't be any forgiving, not this time. I forgave you once, now I can't do it again. You should know you've made an unforgivable mistake. And now it's time for you to pay back." Sahas rose.

"Please Sahas," Dayanand leapt off the couch to touch his son's face, but the frozen look on his face stopped him. How could he make his son understand that he didn't do it because he had a history of being manipulative or was coldblooded? He just loved his son, loved him madly to the extent that even if he felt a speck of anguish, he would not tolerate it. In fact, it would turn him into a demon. But what he hadn't realized was that sometimes abundant, maniac love can get out of control, just the way it happened with him.

Sahas stood on his feet, glanced around the drawings miserably. No matter what, nothing could restore his faith and change the wild decision he had already taken. How could Dayanand even dare to think that he could touch his friend, his best friend, without Sahas intervening to save him?

He turned to him for the last time, wiped the tears of Dayanand and cupped his face, "You thought you were playing the best game ever, but what you never know is, I'm the one going to check mate your move forever. It's your reward. I love you dad. Miss You." He kissed the top of his head before he swung back and sped out of the room.

He shut the door and stood there with his eyes shut, tears leaking from both sides, listening to Dayanand's fists banging the door and shouts for forgiveness. "Please come back, my son... "Please maul me to chainsaw forever, but don't leave me, I can't imagine a life without you."

Sahas kissed the door, his breath fogging. "I'm sorry dad, forgive me." He stood there until the sounds of his father crying bitterly subsided and scooted out of the house.

Inside the room, Dayanand slowly got to his feet, feeling dizzy and looked at the drawings through blurred eyes. It was pure delight to see his son during his childhood days. Sahas was right when he said that he had never been there in his life. It was his friend who had been by his side through thick and thin. Dayanand was so immersed in his business, building up his empire that he had never tried to have a meaningful relationship with his son. He realized what a huge mistake he had committed by taking such a cruel decision. But it was too late now.

Tears streaming down, he staggered around the room, looking for his mobile. He had to stop the goons before things slipped out of his hand. But he couldn't find it. He then went to the land phone and was puzzled to see that it had been disconnected. Someone had deliberately unplugged all the connections. Everything made sense now. No servants, no phones. He was trapped inside. Suddenly Sahas' words struck him.

"Okay, if you can think that relationships can be sustained with bloodstained hands, then let me try one." What did he mean by that? Dayanand collapsed on the floor, his heart thudding in fear. He lifted his head up and let out a scream. Soon, his eyes drifted to sleep, his body turning numb as he collapsed on the floor, unaware of the sleeping pills he was fed in the food.

Sahas walked down the road in the dark, his head lowered. The strong breeze stirred about the plants and trees, indicating heavy rain at anytime. He kept walking along the vast openness, his mind clogged with miserable emotions which he failed to handle like the dust storming in the air. He knew deep inside that things could be sorted out if they were left alone for a while. He could go back anytime, ask his dad to take back his foolish, cruel decision and get back to his friend like before. But he wasn't just thinking about what his dad had done, he was thinking about those thoughts, those wildfire-like thoughts that could scorch a human being's soul to ashes, which he wanted to put a full stop to. In fact, wasn't all this mess a handiwork of him? If only he had never breathed a hatred word about Avinash to his dad. If only Dayanand had never taken such a wild decision. If only he had never hurt Avinash with his volatile behaviour. The bitter words he had spat came back like harsh rain drops and slapped his face, drenching him in the guilt.

"I wish you had died in that accident, Avinash."

Tears rolled down Sahas's cheeks. How could he have even said that? His dad had just planned to kill him, but he had already killed his friend with his razor sharp words. Perhaps they both were the same, Dayanand and Sahas, just different shades from the same colour, selfish colour. Like father, like son.

Sahas uncurled the fingers of his closed palms. Dayanand's mobile that he had secretly slipped into his pocket and a key to Avinash's room sat on it. They always had two keys to Avinash's room, one with his friend and the other with him. Sahas had shoved the key into his suitcase when he had walked out of his friend's room, not having the heart to throw it away.

Now, he tossed Dayanand's mobile into a puddle and began walking briskly, his hands stuffed into the pockets, rain lashing at his face. He headed towards his friend's room. Sahas knew his friend wasn't there and must be lingering around their village, waiting for him with thousand eager eyes. He had deliberately called his friend and made him go to the village. He had wanted to take his friend's place tonight when the goons his dad had hired came to kill him.

As hopeless and daft the decision seemed, Sahas had already trapped into its walls with a firm determination. He could not tell when the idea had taken hold exactly. Perhaps the time when his dad was asking him for forgiveness or when he had glued Avinash's drawings on walls, or even before when he learned the brutal truth from that guy hired by his dad. Whatsoever the timing was, once the idea had taken hold, it never spew out.

Above all, he wanted to destroy his dad's wild thoughts and the person behind those thoughts. Sahas had no clue he was going through a whirlwind of emotions; he could no longer think straight.

Just as he reached, he unlocked the door to the dark, empty room. The memories flooded at him at once. The times, the laughter, the joy, the fights they shared – everything swallowed him up in its huge tide. He longed to see his friend for one last time, hold his hand, ask him for forgiveness and cry on his shoulder. Perhaps it could never be accomplished. Sahas lit a candle and placed it on the table where he found a large portfolio sitting. The sight of it felt like a pail of water to a person who had been lost in the desert for days. He flipped it open, drowning into the charm of the drawings. There were many, and most of them were of Sahas and Avinash.

He took one of the drawings. It was a drawing of the two of them, probably in their teens, sitting on a low cliff facing the waterfalls right in front of them. So real and vivid it looked, he was so engrossed, Sahas had never heard the van pull up by the house. His body became alert only after hearing the footsteps of men striding towards him. He was no more terrified or scared. It was like he was anticipating the moment. Perhaps, this was the punishment he had imposed on himself for not being a good son, friend, or a human being.

Self destruct. This was his decision after all, to lay down his life to make his dad understand that love could not be bought with bloodstained hands. Sahas felt a fierce jab slicing into his ribs. The pain was unbearable as it rippled through his veins, making it impossible for him to breathe. Beads of blood sputtered down to the floor. And yet, he stood tall like an unflinching warrior, his posture suggesting he wanted more. Another stab pierced his ribs. It was more potent than the previous one. His body shook just like the candle fluttered in front of him. His legs felt weak and he could stand no more. He collapsed on the floor and felt his breath slowly leave him. As the goons left, his lips spread in a quirky smile, conveying that he had won by putting an end to his dad's wild thoughts and saving his friend Avinash.

One year later…

It was a beautiful winter morning. Glints of lights washed over the spacious lush and green garden, a place where one could lie beneath a tree and spend a good time. Avinash stood in the large balcony slumping forward, his elbows on the balustrade, probably in the same place where Sahas had often stood and recalled his friend, wordlessly staring at the garden below. Sahas, as humble and insecure was he, but a person full of dreams to claim the world should have lived a long, beautiful life, but his inability to handle inward, emotional turmoil had cut it short. What Avinash could say about those sleepless nights he spent feeling regretful for not having paid much attention to his friend's disquieting sense of vulnerability? Things could never be the same now. He'd feel his absence everywhere around, for he knew he would never get another chance to hug or elbow or punch his friend fondly whenever they shared a happy moment together. Wherever he'd go – the village, or a park or the local pub or in the room, or in his heart where he had shared treasured memories with his friend – he'd find himself thinking about Sahas. It hurt Avinash to think that all those indelible memories that brought a smile to his face would sit until his last breath. But deep inside, he also knew that Sahas would always live in his heart, sharing his soul, looking upon his every action and following him like a shadow wherever he went.

Avinash walked inside the room and dropped beside Dayanand on the bed, where he lay lifeless, his limbs paralyzed. The moment he had learned about his son's death, he had suffered a stroke and was bed-ridden. The left side of his body was of no service anymore. His voice came out in hoarse grunts no one could understand. One could not assimilate the current Dayanand to the strong, impregnable business magnet he once was. Perhaps that was fate's way of making him pay for his mistakes in life. But no matter how lifeless his body was, his eyes turned dewy with a dual burst of gratitude and apology whenever Avinash sat by his side on the bed. Dayanand would repeatedly try and fail to say something as he'd struggle to move his mouth. Though he could never utter anything, Avinash could decipher the simple word the man was trying to convey, 'sorry' perhaps.

Whenever his eyes watered, chin quivered, Avinash would squeeze his motionless hand in genuine concern and tap gently on the wrist. "It's okay," he'd mutter, not able to think of anything better. "Okay, I've got to go now. I'll meet you again soon," Avinash whispered, leaning into Dayanand's ears before tapping his wrist another time. He then rose, slowly shut the door behind and sped down the hall, not before leaving a kind word to the old servant to take good care of his sir. Before climbing onto his bike, he gently tapped his shirt's pocket where a letter lay safe. It was the same letter Sahas had written in tears and asked the servant to post. Avinash carried the letter with him like a shadow. Every single word had been deeply engraved in his heart and there hadn't been a single day when he hadn't read his friend's last letter.

Dearest Avinash,

I offer a thousand prayers that this letter reaches you, no matter what. And I'm sure I won't be in this world when you read this. I know how defeated and depressed you'll be after discovering the ghastly path I've chosen in an attempt to rectify faults. I also know what I am going to lose is irretrievable. But now for me, self destruction was the only option. How should I explain my condition after I learned the awful truth my dad had planned against you. I was so agitated and confused. It was like I was split into two, wavering between wanting to leave him forever and teaching him a lesson. At last, the evil had outgrown forgetfulness. Forgive me if possible for this act Avi, but today I couldn't stop myself from conjuring up those memories that remind me of the days we spent together, having fun. Remember those picturesque waterfalls where we would spend legions of time, splashing and frolicking in the water until my mom came to find us? And remember those long, curvy roads on which you used to take me for a ride, with me sitting on the paddle shrieking 'whoo…'? I was too afraid to even ride a bicycle then. Maybe I was born that way, with fear tied to the umbilical cord. Or perhaps, I was always afraid, anxious about who would take care of my mom if something happened to me.

I don't know!

Today I want to be fearless and bold like a warrior. But before going, you should know something. You are the best gift I have ever been given in my life. Your friendship, your sacrifices, your love – everything that you have given in the name of our friendship is commendable.

And I am sorry, my friend. Sorry for my bitter words, sorry for those misunderstandings, sorry for hurting you and doubting you. But you will never imagine how many times I wished I could take back my words and restore our friendship. I couldn't imagine the plight you have been through. Do you know how strong and kind-hearted god has made you, Avi? You never complained, had no regrets in your life. All you shared with people around was 'love'. It's only possible with you, my dear Avi.

Let me wind up with this. I know how hard it will be for you to accept all this and even harder to cope. But never forget, I'll always be there with you, inside your heart. There may be times when you believe that I am far away, but don't. I will be standing right by your side and smiling at that thought. Whenever you miss me, just look at the stars in the sky and you will surely find one twinkling brightly, saying hi to you.

Avi, you have always been there for me through all my hardships. With the liberty of our friendship, I want to ask you for one last favour. Please take care of my dad. Please keep coming to my home whenever you think of me and see how my dad is doing. I feel ashamed to ask, but please forgive him for his act. He might have made some bad decisions in his life, but he is not a bad person. The insane love he had for me made his thinking brutal. That's all. Thanks for everything.

I miss you and I miss all the laughter, joy, and fun we shared. Killing the urge of seeing you for the last time, I am signing off.

Your best friend, always

Sahas!